ZOONAUTS

THE SECRET OF ANIMALVILLE

FROM BEYOND THE WILD

NEW KINDS OF SUPERHEROES

Richard Mueller

authorHOUSE®

AuthorHouse™
1663 Liberty Drive
Bloomington, IN 47403
www.authorhouse.com
Phone: 1 (800) 839-8640

Published by AuthorHouse 11/11/2015
Edited by Madalyn Abrams
Cover Design by New Show Studios in Pittsburgh, Pennsylvania

ISBN: 978-1-4969-6280-5 (sc)
ISBN: 978-1-4969-6281-2 (hc)
ISBN: 978-1-4969-6279-9 (e)

Library of Congress Control Number: 2015900399

Print information available on the last page.

This book is printed on acid-free paper.

Upcoming sequel in the *Zoonauts* series

Zoonauts: Adventures in China

Other books by Richard Mueller

Jernigan's Egg

Time Machine 24

Ghostbusters: The Supernatural Spectacular

Zoonauts with Jen & Cody Stroud

Dedicated to Cody Simons

In memory of Cathy Lynn

Early in his career David Simons met Patty Cake, the world's most famous gorilla in New York City's Central Park Zoo; this meeting inspired the creation of the Zoonauts adventure series.

CONTENTS

"When you realize the value of all life, you dwell less on what is past and concentrate more on the preservation of the future."

~Dian Fossey

Zoonauts is about our children, the human race,
and the future of our environment on Earth.

PREFACE

WELCOME TO THE EXCITING WORLD OF THE ZOONAUTS!

The *Zoonauts* story is one of animals who save the human race from extinction by a hostile Alien force: the Amadorians.

It is a story written by Richard Mueller, illustrated by Edigio Victor Dal Chele, and conceived by David Simons.

Patty Cake, a Central Park Zoo gorilla, was the inspiration for David Simons to create the *Zoonauts* science fiction adventure series.

Simons commissioned Richard Mueller to compose the story of *Zoonauts*. New Show Studios brought Simons's concept to presentation so the story could be marketed in many languages and developed as an animated series.

Zoonauts is about the love of all creatures great and small. For children, the story is a lesson in the gifts animals and humans possess. *Zoonauts* teaches an appreciation for the bond between Mankind and the Animal Kingdom which protects our peace and planet.

Perhaps Dian Fossey, the world's leading authority on the physiology and behavior of mountain gorillas, said it best when she defined gorillas as "dignified, highly social, gentle giants, with individual personalities, and strong family relationships."

Fossey's last words focused on the future:

"When you realize the value of all life, you dwell less on what is past and concentrate more on the preservation of the future."

~Dian Fossey

Tre-Pok with Kornblend (left) and Fishwick (right)

CHAPTER ONE

WHO ARE THE AMADORIANS?

Fishwick and Kornblend were not happy Amadorians as they reached the Supreme Palace of Amador under the poisonous yellow sky.

The bus that recently delivered Fishwick and Kornblend to the palace had broken down. The Amadorian driver was busy hitting the boiler with a wrench and calling it names. Fishwick and Kornblend ignored him as they stood and stared at the palace.

Calling it a palace was a kindness, although it was certainly large enough. A big ugly rock pile, it reared up against the smoky skies. Amadorian emperors and warlords had been adding to the thing for centuries with no thought as to what it looked like. The result was a lumpy, great building as ugly as any in the Galaxy. It was surrounded by a low city that had a bad reputation and was thick with smoke and machine noises. It was a strip mall Kingdom on a slum of a planet.

Fishwick shook his great scaly head.

"I hate this planet," Fishwick said.

"But this is *our* planet," Kornblend hooted, blowing the soot out of his snout stops.

"I still hate it," said Fishwick. "In the Amadorian Codex Verse XIII, Chapter 27, it specifically states that if you lie down with mud weasels, you'll get up smelling like, well, mud weasels. And that's not so good!"

"Can we get this over with?" Kornblend asked.

A very old Amadorian Palace Guard, leaning on a six-foot-long battle ax weapon, eyed them suspiciously. His scales were painted in a pattern of bile green and yellow. He looked like he'd been standing guard at the palace for a hundred years.

"What do you two bozos want?" the Palace Guard asked with his jaw creaking.

"We have an appointment," said Kornblend.

"What?" asked the Palace Guard. He was hard of hearing.

"We have an appointment," repeated Kornblend.

"What? Speak up. Don't whisper," said the Palace Guard. He was apparently deaf.

"We have an appointment you old fish bag!" Kornblend bellowed. "Let us in!"

Instead, the Palace Guard leveled his weapon. Fishwick and Kornblend looked at each other and then at the old Palace Guard. The charge light on his weapon was dark and the battery was missing. Fishwick gently pushed the tip aside and then screamed into the old Palace Guard's ear.

"Fishwick and Kornblend to see His Awfulness," said Fishwick.

"Why didn't you say so?" said the old Palace Guard.

He tossed the useless weapon down and waddled to the intercom. He had to hit it several times before a red light came on.

"Fishwick and Kornblend are here," he shouted.

With a loud click, the massive doors swung open. Thrusting the old Palace Guard aside, Kornblend strode through the Palace. Fishwick followed, letting out a large sigh.

The palace interior was no better than its exterior. Fishwick and Kornblend had been there many times and were familiar with the protocol. They strode down the corridor and dragged their fat tails. At the end of the corridor, the two dragons came to a door. In the manner of old partners and all soldiers, they scowled and tidied up each other's uniforms.

"Well, you look like crap," said Kornblend.

"Speak for yourself, Kornface," replied Fishwick.

"Why do you think he wants to see us?" asked Kornblend.

"Probably to give me a medal," Fishwick growled.

"You? For what?" asked Kornblend.

"For putting up with you, you dumb iguana," said Fishwick.

Amadorians all look a bit like dragons, but Fishwick was the taller and looked like the sneakier of the two. Kornblend's squat brutishness marked him as the tough guy. They were dressed in shabby Amadorian fighter pilot gear with uniform badges.

Above them a robotic eye swiveled around to look at them. Tre-Pok's voice suddenly blasted out from all sides around them and he was not amused. Tre-Pok was the High General and Chief Warlord.

"Fishwick! Kornblend! Get in here!" said Tre-Pok.

Fishwick and Kornblend stumbled into Tre-Pok's Strategy Room and tripped over their tails, before they landed in a heap on the floor. They untangled themselves and staggered to their feet.

"Get up!" screamed Tre-Pok.

"Yes, Your Awfulness," saluted the two pilots, thumping their chests Roman-style.

Tre-Pok glared at them. He was decked out in leather, medals, and attitude! Some medals were directly attached to his scales. Some scales were covered with shiny metal plates. He examined the two pilots as if he had found them on his boot.

"I've got a job for you two mouth-breathers," Tre-Pok ordered. "And I want it done right!"

"Yesssir!" responded Kornblend and Fishwick together.

"Silence! You are using up my air!" Tre-Pok said. He stalked to his command console.

Fishwick and Kornblend trailed behind him as he stabbed a button on the console. A huge screen dropped from the ceiling and narrowly missed Fishwick who yelped involuntarily.

Kornblend clamped his hands around Fishwick's jaws in the hope that Tre-Pok hadn't heard, but the High General and Chief Warlord of Amador was busy banging his scaly fist on a projector dome. Suddenly, the screen lit up with a picture of Earth. Tre-Pok gave a satisfied grunt.

"I want you to go to Earth," Tre-Pok said. "I trust you remember where it is?"

He twirled around to face the two pilots who nodded vigorously. The image of Earth on the Command Console faded into an image of a Siberian Husky named Laika that the Russians had sent into space years ago.

"Bring back this creature alive and well," bellowed Tre-Pok.

"Alive and well…" repeated Kornblend.

Fishwick elbowed Kornblend.

"Owww," Kornblend cried out. "How do we find him, Your Fearfulness?"

"Use the genetic sensors we provided you with, Bonehead," replied Tre-Pok. "Do a good job!"

Tre-Pok's angry response frightened them. He sat down in a large, creaking chair and looked at the two quaking pilots.

"If you do, there could be medals and another stripe for each of you," promised Tre-Pok. "If you don't, then we might have the same sort of problems here as we did with those blood-sucking plants from Veratex."

The two scout pilots turned white. They remembered what they had heard about that dreadful bloodbath. They saluted so hard they almost broke the bones in their chests.

"Now, get out of here!" Tre-Pok screamed.

The two pilots were out through the door with a slam before Tre-Pok's words finished ringing in the filthy air.

Tre-Pok frowned at them as they left but didn't notice the curtains move behind him as the High Rotocaster slipped into the Strategy Room. The Supreme Spiritual Advisor to the Emperor of Amador, the High Rotocaster had been around so long that no one remembered his name – only that he had somehow survived the Veratex disaster. He was now a spooky dragon, so skinny that he looked like a skeleton. His scales were translucent so that you could almost see through them, but not quite completely. His eyes were red and his voice unworldly—an equivalent of Shakespeare's ghost in *Hamlet*. When the High Rotocaster cleared his throat, it sounded as if someone was eating lightbulbs.

"Sir, Ahhhhh," said Tre-Pok with a startled jump and bow.

"This had better work," said the High Rotocaster. He stared into the distance, immersed deeply in his own thoughts. He would do so frequently which caused Tre-Pok distress and drove him crazy.

Tre-Pok nodded, but the High Rotocaster's attention was focused on the picture of Laika on the command console.

"I must find their weaknesses," commanded The High Rotocaster. "We can *not* afford another mistake."

"I shall not fail the Emperor," Tre-Pok promised. Secretly, he had his doubts.

CHAPTER TWO

METHUSELAH'S TALE

Methuselah, the Stroud family parrot, sat in the scrub oak outside Mrs. Patruski's eighth-grade class and listened to Jennifer Stroud present her assignment.

"That was a very creative story, Jennifer, but I think we have heard enough right now about Amador and silly space dragons!" interrupted Mrs. Patruski.

"You were *instructed* to write a story involving something that happened to your family, not science fiction, or worse, fantasy!"

"But…," began Jen. (Jen was her nickname. Everyone called her Jen except Mrs. Patruski.)

Mrs. Patruski waved her to silence.

"If I give the whole class an assignment, I expect *all* of you to do it," said Mrs. Patruski. "This assignment was not just about writing anything you felt like writing."

Mrs. Patruski glared at Jennifer.

Jen tried to hide her anger and embarrassment and her urge to say something. She thought anything she might say would only make matters worse. Mrs. Patruski made Jen so nervous that she just sank back into her chair without a word.

It was already turning into a bad spring term and it was still only February. Jen just knew what her brother Cody would say when she got home: "I told you so." "How could you be so dumb?" "When are you going to learn?"

Cody was three years younger, but he always had a better sense of what "outsiders" might understand about their strange family. It made it so hard to have any friends when you couldn't tell them anything about your home.

Jen reflected on the truth of her circumstances. Truth number one: No child had ever grown up in the kind of family like the Strouds. While their nonhuman nursemaids cared for them and taught them things no human child had learned, Jen was tired of telling other girls that they couldn't visit her home. While she often went to their homes to study, usually some animal would watch everything she did. She always felt like she was scrutinized and, at times, the lack of privacy was too much to bear. Jen felt very gloomy as she left school that day.

"What was that weird story all about?" asked Sara, Jen's best friend. Sara interrupted Jen's thoughts as the two walked home from school.

"Oh, just something Methuselah the Parrot told me," Jen blurted out. Afterwards she realized what she had said.

"You're bonkers, Jen!" said Sara. "Next you're going to tell me you know why the Space Shuttle Columbia blew up over Texas!"

"Oh, Sara!" cried Jen.

Jen started to cry harder than she ever had before.

"It's just awful! I've got to tell somebody, or I'll burst," said Jen.

"Tell me!" said Sara.

"Can you keep a secret?" asked Jen.

Sara nodded.

"I mean a *real* secret," said Jen. "Not just something dumb!"

"Of course, silly!" said Sara. "Duh!"

"Sara, I need to tell you something, but can't," said Jen, as she pulled herself together and wiped away the tears. She realized that telling Sara anything was both dangerous and useless, yet she had to show her!

"Sara, I need to let you in on the secret of Animalville, but don't know how. Let's go find Methuselah. He is a real smart bird and may have an idea!"

Sarafina Flores-Abaroa just knew that Jen had had too many marshmallow cream pies for lunch and thought Jen was just experiencing a sugar high.

"Ready, Jen?" called Mrs. Stroud, as she pulled up in the car to give the girls a ride home.

"Hi, Mom," Jen greeted her. "Where's our regular driver?"

"He is on a special mission today dealing with a crash," said Mrs. Stroud.

"Mom, can Sara come home today since there is no one around to report us?" asked Jen.

"You know the rules, Jen," warned Mrs. Stroud.

"But... Mommmmm!" Jen pleaded.

"No, and that's final!" said Mrs. Stroud.

"Then let me walk home, so Sara and I can spend more time together," Jen pleaded.

"OK, but don't be too late!" said Mrs. Stroud.

While they were talking, Cody arrived. He climbed into the car and they drove off.

"Jen, don't feel too bad," Sara confided. "At least you have a real family! Grandma Camille is all I have since my mom ran off to 'find herself' in Utah. She doesn't understand half of what goes on since she only speaks Spanish."

"I know, but sometimes they are just too 'real' and they always watch us," said Jen. She recalled how difficult it had been to communicate with Sara's Grandmother Camille when she tried to thank her for the authentic Mexican dinner she had prepared for them that was such a great treat!

"I guess they love you," Sara almost whispered. "I wish I had that."

The girls said almost nothing as they walked on through the quiet streets near the edge of town. There, past the last house, squatting behind the fence, was Animalville.

A huge statue of Texas Bob cast its long shadow across the road where the military guard shack stood. The road disappeared down a tunnel. Jen traveled the road daily, but none of her friends had ever been through the tunnel, not even Sara.

"Wait for me there, Sara, and I'll be right back," said Jen. She pointed to a stand of cottonwood trees near the entrance.

"OK," said Sara.

Sara sat under the tree and watched Jen wave to soldiers in the guard shack as she disappeared down the tunnel. About 10 minutes elapsed. Sara started to get nervous. Suddenly, Cody showed up from nowhere.

"Oh, it's you!" said Sara. "Say, what's wrong with Jen?"

Sara questioned Cody and shook off her surprise at Cody's arrival. She imagined herself a secret agent, but had no idea how close she was to learning a real *top secret*.

"Nothing!" said Cody. "What do you mean?"

"Jen told some crazy science-fiction story in school today about another planet with dragons…she said something weird about the story…that it was one of your parrots that told her the story…then she just burst into tears," explained Sara.

Cody rolled his eyes as only a nine-year-old brother can.

"Women!" said Cody emphatically. "Now we're in for it!"

At that precise moment, Jen rounded the corner of the cottonwoods with Methuselah the Parrot perched on her shoulder.

Sara eyed the old bird and the thought crossed her mind: "What if Jen *was* telling the *truth*?"

"What have you done?" Cody cried. "I told you they wouldn't understand about Amador. I told you so!"

Cody disappeared and ran into the tunnel like the White Rabbit in *Alice and Wonderland*.

The guards totally ignored him as they had seen the Stroud children argue before.

Jen and Sara looked knowingly at each other. Sara realized Jen was right about one thing: her brother Cody was, at times, a pain.

Suddenly Methuselah spoke.

"Jen, Cody is right! Your Amador report was a big mistake. A big mistake!" said Methuselah.

As far as Sara was concerned, the impossible had just occurred. Methuselah had spoken—not in just parrot-speak—but like a real human.

"Excuse me, Sara, given my language gifts, the other animals here in Animalville have chosen me to be their spokes-being," said Methuselah. He keenly sensed Sara's amazement.

"What I am about to tell you is, of course, a *top secret* – a military secret. *Do you know what that means*?" asked Methuselah.

Sara nodded in disbelief and stared at Methuselah.

"Good!" Methuselah continued. "Because with that secret comes the *responsibility* of never telling anyone else...*and* if you do, *terrible* things could happen to Jen...to you...and to *all of us*....So if you don't want to know..."

Sara was scared and her mouth was dry, but she was excited beyond words. She was totally amazed at Methuselah's admission and wanted to know this secret more than anything in the world.

"I-I-I won't tell anyone," Sara stammered. "I want to know."

"Very well," said Methuselah. "This is a report about a war between Earth and Amador. I will tell you the story of how Animalville came to be. I am older than most anyone and remember these things. I know how we came here and how we are saving the world."

"You mean there are other talking animals besides you?" Sara exclaimed.

"After hearing my story, you'll never look at animals the same way again," said Methuselah. "But if you will listen hard and wait for one of us to speak in your language, you know what? We just might!"

"Of course," interrupted Jen. "You won't look at the sky the same way either because there are things up there, flying just above our heads, that did not come from Earth. Strange creatures from another planet are waiting to conquer us, just like I said in my school paper!"

"Excuse me, Jen, but I was giving this lecture!" Methuselah said in a disturbed tone.

"Who else knows about this?" asked Sara. She was more than a little shocked while she waited for Methuselah's reply.

"Well, the President of the United States, the US Air Force, NASA, and other special people," said Methuselah.

His feathers were puffed out, and he tipped his head back to gather his thoughts.

"Some are humans, others are dogs, cats, birds, mice, monkeys, gorillas, pandas, even koalas," Methuselah mused. "I realize this is a lot for you to understand all at once, but..."

"You're not kidding?" Sara exclaimed.

"Hah! Have you ever heard a parrot talk like me?" asked Methuselah with a chuckle.

"Well...no," admitted Sara.

"Please, get comfortable. I will tell you a story so amazing that you may not be able to sleep," promised Methuselah. "In fact, you may never want to sleep again!"

Jen and Sara focused on the old gray parrot Methuselah as they rested under the cottonwoods near the fence that surrounded Animalville. The cool breeze ruffled the grass on that sunny day as Methuselah told Sara the secret of Animalville.

Methuselah began:

"After the last great human World War – called the Second World War – the world was left with two great and powerful nations: America, also known as the United States, and Russia. There were many other nations, but my story is about America and Russia – the superpowers."

"I don't remember any of that," said Sara.

"Superpowers are large countries with many creatures and lots of ways to make the lives of their people better. But they distrust, envy, and consider each other evil. That is dangerous because with the terrible weapons they possess, a war between them could become the last one," explained Methuselah.

"Humans were frightened. Air raid sirens blew. Children crouched under their desks and waited for terrible bombs. It was very frightening! To make it less scary, the exercises to prepare for the conflict were called something that even sounded like a game: 'Duck and Cover'," Methuselah explained.

"Was it like our 'lock in place' drills after September 11th?" asked Jen.

"Sort of, but not exactly," said Methuselah. "You were not born yet! At that time, I watched and wondered if everyone had gone crazy... perhaps they had and it's happening all over again."

"How did we survive back then?" asked Sara.

"Luckily, there were a few sane humans," said Methuselah. "It was called the 'Cold War' because it was potentially a dangerous situation which, like dynamite, might explode if it got too hot."

"Smart humans realized that if leaders weren't given something to do, they would argue and then we would have a Third World War. America and Russia needed to compete, but not fight – although the Olympics are nice, they were held only every four years. There was culture—while Russians had ballet, the Americans had television—but that was not a solution! Humans needed a difficult, dangerous, and distant place to keep quarrelsome people very busy. With all the lands on Earth discovered, 'The Wild West' tamed, and Africa explored, there were no more mysteries here on Earth," said Methuselah. "So, then a very smart human looked up to the sky and said: 'Let's explore space!' It was a perfect solution as there are countless stars and planets to explore, but people first needed a way to escape gravity."

"So we made rockets!" Sara exclaimed.

"Yes, humans had been flying for a long time, even before the Second World War. Did I mention I was in that War?" asked Methuselah in a self-deprecating way.

"Not yet," Jen said with a yawn. "But I am sure you will eventually… you always do!"

"Well…yes…people flew more than 40,000 feet up into the sky, over seven miles; however, space is millions of miles. They needed a new way to fly. You are right, Sara. They made rockets, but found they weren't too safe, so they decided to first send animals."

"How do you know all this?" Sara asked.

"Simple truth: I was one of the first! If animals died in space, they could try again, but if we lived, humans would follow," explained Methuselah.

"This sounds cruel," Methuselah continued. "However, dogs, cats, horses, and even birds have been helping humans for thousands of years. We often share dangers with humans. Dogs protect your flocks, cats keep houses free from rats, horses carry you, and birds deliver messages and sing for you. When humans began to send animals into space, the animals were afraid, but the animals were also proud. Space changed us forever, although at first humans didn't notice."

"What do you mean?" asked Sara, puzzled.

"I was the first animal to change, but I have not been in Space since I was thirty years old. When the Space Program started, I was too old to go. Instead, I lived at the Cape Canaveral base in Houston and watched other animals go into space," Methuselah explained.

"So how old are you anyway?" Sara asked.

"I am over eighty years now," answered Methuselah.

"But how did you change?" asked Sara.

"That is a long story," said Methuselah.

CHAPTER THREE
A SMART, OLD BIRD

Methuselah puffed out his feathers with pride.

"Methuselah is a name that means *very old*. It is true. Look it up," said Methuselah. "I was never in space, as I said, because I was already too old for the space program."

"So what changed you?" Sara pressed for answers as she was getting more curious about this strange old bird.

"Aliens changed me in 1952!" Methuselah blurted out.

"Ahhhh, yes," he sighed. "My story with humans started in 1944 when I was already in my teens and living in a West African Jungle in Ghana. You see, I am a Senegal Gray Parrot who was named after the Senegal River. We are smart birds although I was destined to get a lot smarter. However, it took something very stupid to occur first!"

"What was that?" asked Sara.

"There was plenty to eat in the jungle, but near the edge of town there was a flat clearing called an *airport*. It was the US Army Air Corps Base at Takoradi, but I did not know that then," explained Methuselah.

"Large airplanes came from the West across the Atlantic Ocean and landed there. Men did things to the planes and then flew them east to never return. I found out later they were coming to Takoradi from the United States by way of Brazil, but these planes were heading east to Egypt and China and a war."

"At the time, I was interested only in plums…ripe, succulent plums," Methuselah mused.

"I don't get the connection," Sara admitted.

"The men in Takoradi were refueling and checking airplanes to make sure they were fit to fly. Birds do these things naturally, but you humans are not designed to fly, so you build airplanes. I never saw airplanes before on the ground, only flying in the jungle. I was to see more airplanes, but at that time, I was only interested in plums."

"So?" Sara asked, getting impatient.

"You see, there was a plum tree on the air base. I could see it from my jungle perch, and it grew by a window of a building I learned later was the Transient Aircrew Barracks where flight crews slept between flights," Methuselah elaborated. "Humans can't perch in trees as we birds do, but plums…wonderful sweet plums were all that captured my attention. I determined that I must have them."

"I flew from the jungle over a fence and straight to the plum tree, where I ate the most wonderful fruit. I decided that the plums were so good that I planned to do it every day. I flew to the plum tree for the next 10 days until I noticed there were other plums missing beside those I had eaten!"

"Humans apparently like plums too! The human who tended this tree had seen me fly there. His name was Sergeant Otis Fox. He was able to trick me because he was smarter than I was then. So on my eleventh flight to the plum tree, I heard a snapping sound. Sergeant Fox caught me in a net. Afterwards I lived in a cage in his room in the Transient Aircrew Barracks."

"It must be awful to be in a cage," Sara said.

"Well," Methuselah replied, "There are worse things, but it wasn't the most pleasant experience."

"Go on," Jen said impatiently.

"Very well," said Methuselah, shaking his head and muttering, "Human children can be so impatient. Well, let's see, where was I? Ahhh, yes, Sergeant Otis Fox. He was in charge of the barracks and now he was in charge of me. I must admit he treated me well although he made me stay in a cage. I hated the cage, but he gave me seeds and fruit to eat – even plums. He talked to me and got me to talk back to him. That is all I could do then because that is what normal parrots do. I didn't understand much, but I did say what he asked me to repeat. After a time, he clipped my wings and let me out of the cage so I could not fly away. Sometimes, I rode around on his shoulder while he worked. Other times, he let me sit on a perch at his door."

"Wait a minute," interrupted Sara. "How can you fly now if Sergeant Fox cut your wings?"

"Oh, my feathers grow back every year! Aren't birds great? The transient aircrews who flew the airplanes would talk to me and feed me. Sometimes, they would even get me to say things I shouldn't!" said Methuselah with a smile. "I now know what those words mean, so I shall not repeat them to you; however, then I did not know. Poor language sent me to China."

Jen and Sara giggled.

"It's true. One day I was sitting on my perch and as I chewed a plum, the General came in. Had I known better, I would not have called him a 'fat a** desk jockey.' I didn't know what that meant, of course, but he certainly did!"

"So what did he do?' asked Sara. "Your wings were already clipped!"

"The red-faced General found Sergeant Otis Fox and told him that he would send him to Greenland if I was not off the base by sundown," said Methuselah. "Greenland is apparently not as nice a place as it sounds, so Sergeant Fox gave me to a transient pilot, Major Mike McIntosh."

"Wait a minute," said Sara. "Why didn't you just fly back to the jungle or somewhere?"

"Well, with my wings clipped, I couldn't fly. Instead, I was put back in a cage in a B-29 bomber plane heading east to join the B-29 High-Flying Fifinella aircrew."

"What happened next and how did you get out of the cage?" said Sara.

The aircrew was good to me. I got to know them as we flew to Cairo, Egypt. Then we flew to Bombay, India. Finally we reached China. I missed my jungle, but was well fed. I found it wasn't too bad an experience with all the exciting adventures I experienced. In fact, I considered myself a lucky bird. The crew thought so as well and wanted me on their missions."

"I looked dashing, and we would fly high where there is thin or almost no air. During flights from Africa to China, when we were low enough, we didn't need oxygen. On these missions, we went up to 30,000 feet (5 1/2 miles). I was the first parrot to fly so high. We flew a number of missions and had many adventures, but then the war ended. Major Mike stayed in the Army Air Corps and it later became the US Air Force. I stayed with him."

"But how did you get so smart?" asked Sara.

"I am getting to that...," promised Methuselah.

SPACE MILESTONE TIME LINE – 1950s

- In **1944**, Germany developed a liquid fuel rocket called V-2. Instead of using it in space, the Germans shot explosive warheads at Great Britain but still lost the war. The United States brought back many V-2 rockets.
- In **1945**, White Sands Proving Ground, New Mexico, was opened for rocket research.
- In **1946**, a US-launched V-22 rocket carried a spectrograph 34 miles high to study the sun.
- In **1947**, a US jet plane broke the sound barrier for the first time piloted by Captain Chuck Yeager.
- In **1949**, a rocket test ground was set up at Cape Canaveral. At White Sands, the first two-stage rocket flew up 240 miles.
- In **1955**, the United States began the Vanguard Project for launching artificial satellites.
- In **1957**, Russia (formerly the Soviet Union) launched its first artificial satellite, Sputnik I, and launched a second satellite carrying a live dog, **Laika**.
- In **1958**, the first US Vanguard satellite went into orbit.
- In **1959**, the Russians put a satellite (Lunik) in orbit around the sun and crash-landed a rocket (Lunik II) on the moon. Lunik III then photographed the dark side of the moon.
- Also in **1959**, **Miss Baker**, a squirrel monkey who was called America's "First Lady in Space," flew into space on a US Jupiter rocket and returned safely to Earth.

CHAPTER FOUR

MUCH SMARTER

"**M**ost parrots learn to say things like: 'Polly wants a cracker,' or 'Who's a pretty boy?' but you are really smart!" said Sara.

"Yes," Methuselah agreed, "I do have a considerably larger vocabulary."

"Fewer ten dollar words," groaned Jennifer.

"OK, so I use big words. Get over it!" Methuselah urged her. "As for snacks, I prefer almond croissants or a pastry called bear claws. Where was I? I digress. We were talking about intelligence, right?"

"Right," echoed Sara.

"Right," echoed Jen.

"By 1950, a war broke out in Korea. Major Mike and his aircrew took off in the 'High–Flying Fifinella II.' It was a new B-29 aircraft with the same name as his old plane. They were assigned to an island named Chengdu, South Korea. I went with them. By that time, I had traveled nearly halfway around the world with our aircrew. They had flown more than forty missions in two wars without anyone getting hurt! They said that I was their good luck charm!"

Sara and Jen managed a smile.

"Were you popular?" asked Sara.

"Everyone at the base visited me, even the General-in-Charge who I did not call any names!" boasted Methuselah. "We flew 'photographic reconnaissance.' This meant we flew over Korea and took pictures. We never dropped any bombs. I didn't think much about that then, but now I'm happy about it. I don't like the idea of killing a friend or an enemy."

"But how did you get so smart?" asked Sara.

"I am getting to that! We were flying back from the Yalu River after the crew took their pictures. Everyone was relaxed. Suddenly, a hole appeared in the wall next to my cage. Then more holes started to appear. A MIG-15 fighter airplane was coming after us and shot at us."

"Oh my God!" cried Sara and Jen. They looked at each other in alarm.

"So, Major Mike put the High–Flying Fifinella II into a climb. We went up, higher, farther, and faster than ever before. We lost the MIG-15 in a cloud at about 33,000 feet, which is about six miles up in the sky. That is when *it* happened," said Methuselah.

"*It*?" Sara asked.

"Shhhh," Jen whispered. "I love this part!"

"The plane was flooded with a bright yellow light. It seemed like it was coming from the walls. A crewman yelled that we were dead. That was all I remembered until later," said Methuselah.

"When I woke up, the plane was flying, but I didn't hear the crew. I opened my cage which was a task I had not been able to accomplish before. Then I walked up to the cockpit where the aircrew controls the plane," said Methuselah. "Everyone was asleep. When I looked out through the round windows, I saw the ocean below. In fact, the ocean was much too close."

"Did you crash?" asked Sara.

"I perched on Major Mike's shoulder and banged my very hard curved beak on his forehead until he woke up," said Methuselah.

"'What the devil?' he said. Then he asked, 'Where are we?' Then he started to yell to wake the aircrew. Everyone took their post. Eventually, we gradually gained altitude and made it back to the base."

"Were you a hero?" asked Sara.

"I returned to my cage, and listened...," explained Methuselah.

"Were you scared?" Sara asked.

"I was very scared," admitted Methuselah. "Suddenly, though, I understood English. That yellow light did something. While it made us fall asleep, it also boosted my brainpower. I had changed. I was smarter than most humans. I was smart enough not to tell anyone what had happened. I continued to talk like a normal parrot even when they gave me a medal for saving the High–Flying Fifinella II aircrew!"

"What happened next?" asked Sara.

"Well, the Korean War ended. Major Mike McIntosh was promoted to lieutenant colonel and he brought me to the United States."

"You are a hero!" exclaimed Sara.

Major Mike McIntosh with Methuselah
Cape Canaveral, Florida

CHAPTER FIVE

THE SPACE RACE

"**S**ara, do you remember the Space Race I told you about?" asked Methuselah.

"Yes," replied Sara.

When it started, Colonel Mike was assigned to it and of course, he took me with him," said Methuselah. "At first, Colonel Mike was assigned to fly B-29 aircraft that were used to train test pilots like Chuck Yeager."

"Yes, the guy with the 'right stuff,'" said Sara.

"Yes, the very same," said Methuselah. "When that phase of testing was complete, and Yeager broke the sound barrier, Colonel Mike was reassigned from base-to-base. I learned that Colonel Mike's mission was to organize a space program that used animals in experiments and to supervise their human caretakers."

"That was a good thing?" Sara asked uncertainly.

"Well, to tell you the truth, I was worried about this because I had been reading Colonel Mike's magazines when he was out. I learned how animals were used to test medicines and cosmetics," said Methuselah.

"Awww, geez," said Sara and Jen with empathy. "Were you afraid?"

"Many animals were hurt. I read about hunting and people abandoning cats and dogs. This made me furious," said Methuselah. "I was depressed, you might say, so I stopped eating and talking. I even began pulling out my feathers."

"Good thing they grow back!" said Sara.

"Colonel Mike became very upset and fussed over me," Methuselah explained. "He bought me sweet plums, special seeds, and Brazil nuts. He talked to me and scratched my neck. That is when I realized the *truth*."

"What *truth*?" asked Sara.

"Many people, like Colonel Mike, are good to animals," Methuselah stated with relief. "They even love their pets and take great care of them. Some even go without food themselves to pay for medicine for their dogs, cats, and birds. Others arrange organizations to protect animals and volunteer at shelters or rescue societies. Humans, can be very confusing. I was destined to live with them, so I decided to help the best of them and see what good I might accomplish!"

Sara and Jen smiled.

"I can tell, Sara, that you're one of those good humans," Methuselah said with a wink. "That's part of the reason I'm letting you in on this secret."

Sara nodded, but didn't say anything in response.

"Colonel Mike and I had been working with chimpanzees that were in a program to test gravity and its effects," said Methuselah. "The chimpanzees were strapped into machines called centrifuges and whirled around at great speed. It made them feel very heavy, the same way I felt when Major Mike climbed very fast in the B-29."

"Did the chimps get sick?" asked Sara.

"Many chimpanzees became sick. Some died," said Methuselah, somberly. "I thought that strange because I had known chimpanzees back in Africa who were very strong. So, I began watching them while Colonel Mike was doing other things. They talked to one another inside their cages. I realized they were lonely. They needed to touch, groom, and exercise. I felt they were in prison. I guess they were, but I also realized that I understood their language."

"Did they talk to you?" asked Sara.

"Well, one day I began talking to them. They all got so excited at hearing a bird speak in Chimpanzee that they all started to screech," said Methuselah. "The humans in charge of the lab came running to see what was causing all the excitement. I played dumb and acted like I had no idea."

"Did they ever talk back to you?" asked Jen.

"I tried to talk to them several times after that," said Methuselah. "For a long time, they just got excited and screeched and shook the bars. Then one female, named Sheba the Chimpanzee answered."

"'How can you speak our language?' Sheba asked," explained Methuselah.

"What did you say? Did you tell her about the yellow light?" asked Sara.

"I found out first what was wrong with the chimpanzees," said Methuselah. "No one understood that for the chimpanzees to be happy, they needed to groom each other, play, and exercise. That was a big problem; I had to break the news to Colonel Mike."

"How did you do it? I mean, break the news?" Jen piped in.

"After dinner that night, while watching *The Twilight Zone* on television, Colonel Mike was sitting in his easy chair reading about chimpanzee behavior. I was sitting on my perch pretending to be interested in a Brazil nut," explained Methuselah. "Actually, I was worrying about how to break the news to him that I could really talk. I thought he might think he was going crazy since humans often think they are going crazy if something happens they don't understand. One would think they would study the new thing; instead, they often blame themselves first. Humans can be such a confusing species!"

"So, how did you break the news?" asked Sara.

"Well, just then Colonel Mike looked off into space and muttered to himself: 'I don't know! I don't get it! We really know so little about animals!'" Methuselah recalled.

"'You're a smart bird, Methuselah, so what do you think?' he said. He looked straight at me and his question made my reply easy," said Methuselah.

"'Think about what, Colonel Mike?' I replied," Methuselah said.

"What was his reaction?" asked Jen and Sara, laughing.

"His eyes widened and he dropped his book. He stared at me. I realized, without thinking, I had answered him out loud," explained Methuselah. "We looked at each other, and I was the first animal who had become as intelligent as humans. I was the first who could really talk. Colonel Mike was about to become the first human to know this, so I had to be very careful so that he wouldn't think he had lost his mind."

"What did he say?" asked Sara.

"'You can talk?' Colonel Mike said quietly. He sounded hoarse and I think he was frightened," said Methuselah. "I remembered the moment in the B-29 when I first understood human speech and I was also frightened, so I knew how he was feeling."

"What did you say to him?" asked Jen.

"I told him that lots of birds talk," said Methuselah.

"But not like you," Sara argued.

"True! That's the same thing he said to me, Sara," explained Methuselah. "I looked at him. He looked back at me and asked me, 'Who are you?'"

"'Hello, I'm Methuselah, the Gray Senegalese Parrot,' I told him," explained Methuselah. "'You brought me here from Africa years ago.'"

"'I haven't been drinking,' Colonel Mike muttered to himself. 'I don't drink, but maybe I should start. Maybe I have been working too hard,' he said," Methuselah recounted.

"Colonel Mike didn't drink alcohol then because he could not fly since it makes humans act foolishly and their heads hurt," explained Methuselah. "One crewman on the High–Flying Fifinella once gave me some beer. It tasted like dead beetles that had been left in a puddle of water too long. I don't know what they see in it."

"Drinking is pretty awful," agreed Jen.

"Yes," added Sara, "It scares me when adults drink."

The two girls had discussed this subject before.

"Well, Colonel Mike did not drink. He was quite normal, so I tried to calm him down and explain that I was different and changed. I was much smarter than I was before," Methuselah explained.

"'How smart are you?' Colonel Mike asked me," Methuselah said. "So I answered the question exactly because I had read his books and magazines when he was out."

"How smart are you?" asked Sara.

"In human terms, I have an IQ of 145!" explained Methuselah matter-of-factly.

"That's impossible!" exclaimed Sara.

"That is just what Colonel Mike said. 'Impossible.' That is a standard human reaction to anything humans don't understand. How you humans ever learned to fly with that attitude is beyond me, but somehow you muddled through," said Methuselah with scorn.

"Nevertheless, it is true," Methuselah replied. "For a couple of minutes, we looked at each other before Colonel Mike began to test me with a long string of questions."

"'Who is President?' Colonel Mike asked. 'John F. Kennedy,' I replied," said Methuselah.

"'What does NASA stand for?' he asked," said Methuselah.

"'The National Aeronautics and Space Administration,' I replied," Methuselah said.

"'What is the atomic weight of Cesium?' he asked," said Methuselah.

"What is Cesium?" asked Jen, with a twinkle in her eye.

"I'm a parrot, not a chemist, but I could look it up for you if you like," said Methuselah.

"Don't bother; we don't need to know until I take a chemistry class," said Sara so as not to stray from the subject. She had noticed Methusleah often liked to digress from one topic to another.

"Anyway, this Q&A session went on for a while. I thought Colonel Mike was trying to trap me or figure out that I was using a microphone and a speaker to trick him like on the TV show *Candid Camera* he watched," said Methuselah. "Then I realized he was determined to discover just how much I knew. He clearly thought I could not know much since I was a parrot. Finally, he sat back and asked, 'You've been reading, haven't you?'" explained Methuselah.

"I replied, 'Yes,'" said Methuselah. "Then he asked, 'Watching television?' What about radio?" So I replied, 'Yes! Yes!' 'What else?' he asked, so I admitted that I remember all I see since memory was my gift."

"You didn't remember Cesium," Jen said smugly.

"That's true," said Methuselah. "It's one thing to remember everything; it's another to organize it in your head to find it at the moment someone else asks!"

Methuselah raised a claw and scratched his head feathers and then smoothed them back into shape.

"Then Colonel Mike asked me the big question," said Methuselah. "He asked, 'How did this happen?'"

"'Remember the time when the bright light flooded the B-29 airplane and we all fell asleep?'" recounted the eighty-year-old parrot. "Later, when I woke you up, I could understand what was being said!"

"Then I asked Colonel Mike a question that had bothered me for ten years!" said Methuselah. "'Didn't you change too? What about the other men,' I asked him."

"Colonel Mike seemed disappointed," Methuselah said, smoothing his ruffled feathers. "'I have not changed and have not heard about the other aircrew,' Colonel Mike said. 'Six of them are still alive, so I will ask.' He asked, but none of them had been changed – just me."

"So humans don't change?" Sara asked. "Only the animals?"

"Only the animals as far as I know," Methuselah replied. "Ooops! Awwrk. Polly wants a cracker! Pieces of eight! Kiss the black spot!"

Sara was totally confused by Methuselah's strange outburst.

Jen had seen it all before. It was how Methuselah acted when a human who wasn't in on the secret of Animalville got too close. Jen turned to see the Air Force sergeant from the gate ambling toward them.

"Hi, Sergeant Murphy!" Jen greeted.

"Hi, kids!" Sergeant Murphy replied.

Methuselah had fallen silent. He was scratching his head with his foot. He looked like any other parrot, but kept a close eye on Sergeant Murphy.

"Are you kids alright?" Sergeant Murphy asked. "It's just you are usually home by this time of day."

Jen glanced at the sun sinking toward the horizon. The Sergeant was right.

"It was such a nice day that we thought we would sit outside and enjoy the weather," said Jen with a shrug.

"Hey, that's great," said Sergeant Murphy. "I wish I had a parrot, but I don't think my cat would approve. You kids have a nice time. Good-bye, Polly."

Sergeant Murphy went back to the gatehouse. When he was finally out of earshot, Methuselah made a grumpy, clicking sound.

"Why do all humans insist on calling all parrots 'Polly'? Really?" squawked Methusleah.

Jen and Sara laughed until Methuselah fixed them with his stern gaze.

"If there are no further interruptions," Methuselah began.

"Go on," said Sara. "Please, I want to hear."

"Very well," began Methuselah again. "I asked if Colonel Mike was going to tell NASA and the US Air Force about me. He laughed and said, 'Not unless I am bucking for a Section Eight.'"

"What is a Section Eight?" Sara asked.

"A Section Eight is what the US Air Force calls it when they ask a person with mental health issues to leave," Methuselah replied.

"'Well, I don't think you are crazy,' I told Colonel Mike," said Methuselah. "He replied that was not much comfort coming from a talking bird with an IQ of 145," said Methuselah.

"He told me he was upset because I was a parrot with an IQ of 145, and his IQ was only 142," said Methuselah. "He asked me how I knew my IQ was exactly 145."

"How did you find that out?" asked Sara.

"I sent away for the tests," said Methuselah. "'I write, too!' I told Colonel Mike. He just shook his head. Then he looked at the clock and said, 'It's almost midnight, so let's turn in. We can talk more about this tomorrow.'"

"The next morning, Colonel Mike called in sick," said Methuselah. "We spent the day talking and drinking fruit juice to 'wet our whistles' as he liked to put it. It must be a human thing as my whistle works best when my mouth is dry, but I love fruit juice!"

"What did he tell you?" asked Sara, eager to learn the secrets of Animalville.

"First, we talked about Aliens," said Methuselah.

"Aliens?" Sara said in disbelief, as she rolled her eyes toward the sky and turned her head toward Jen.

"People had been seeing Aliens since the Second World War, or earlier," said Methuselah. "I didn't know then what I know now about Amador, Amadorians, and their plans. If I had known, perhaps things would have developed faster and Animalville would have come about sooner. Humans have a saying: 'There is no use crying over spilled milk.' It means that instead of worrying about what went wrong, start thinking about what to do to make it right. Good advice."

"Since the Russians, Chinese, and Koreans had no weapons like what struck the High-Flying Fifinella II, Colonel Mike and I concluded that Aliens must have done it," said Methuselah. "Colonel Mike had studied something called Project Blue Book, a US Air Force program about Aliens."

"Meanwhile, I talked to the animals and told Colonel Mike what they said. I began with the chimpanzees," said Methuselah. "Colonel Mike made important changes to improve the Zoonauts' lives. He provided better food, bigger cages, regular walks, and other exercises. He was promoted from lieutenant colonel to full colonel and called 'a bird' because he wore eagles on his uniform. I thought this was a funny title, but it was a promotion and an honor. We settled in Cape Canaveral, Florida, where we worked full-time taking care of the animals."

"Colonel Mike wrote reports on animal behavior and conditions. NASA and the US Air Force used these reports to improve the conditions of the lab animals," said Methuselah. "Colonel Mike had less success finding out about Aliens. After he asked too many questions, two men in dark suits, Mr. Valentine and Mr. Christmas, came to the house."

"Yikes!" said Jen.

"What did they do to you?" asked Sara.

"They told Colonel Mike to stop asking questions or his career would be over and he would be in trouble," said Methuselah. "They did not know that I could understand everything. Up until this time, only Colonel Mike and a few other animals knew about me. We decided to keep it that way as long as possible. So when I asked about these two men, Colonel Mike said that they were from NSA, the National Security Agency. It sounds like NASA, but it is the agency that tells you when to stop asking questions. By 1976, we made a great discovery!"

SPACE MILESTONE TIME LINE – 1960S

- In **1961**, **Ham**, a chimpanzee, paved the way for Alan Shepard and Virgil "Gus" Grissom to become the first and second Mercury astronauts in suborbital flights. They splashed down in the Atlantic.

- In **1962**, the US Mariner Spacecraft reached Venus. John Glenn became the first American to orbit Earth. The Telestar Communications Satellite was launched. American Astronaut Scott Carpenter and Wally Schirra orbited Earth.

- In **1963**, Russian Valentine Tereshkova-Nikolayeva became the first woman in space.

- In **1964**, the US Ranger 7 probe took 4,316 pictures of the moon.

- In **1965**, Cosmonaut Aleksi Leonov took the first spacewalk. US Astronauts Virgil Grissom and John Young rode the first two-man Gemini capsule. The Mariner IV Spacecraft reached Mars.

- In **1966**, the Russian probe Luna X became the first to orbit the moon.

- In **1967**, Americans Virgil "Gus" Grissom, Ed White, and Roger Chafee died in the Apollo I spacecraft fire. Surveyor III landed safely on the moon and took pictures and soil samples. The American Mariner V and Russian Venera 4 probes visited Venus. Neil Armstrong became the first human to walk on the moon and famously said, "One giant step for man, one giant leap for mankind."

Methuselah and Biff the Mouse

CHAPTER SIX

NOT ALONE

B y now, Sara was sitting down with a frozen, dazed look on her face. It was all too unbelievable.

"Sara" Jen interrupted. "Are you OK? Would you like something to eat?"

"I guess so, but I know I'm never going to tell anyone about this or they'd lock me up!" Sara interjected. "I guess I am thirsty."

Methuselah smiled.

"Jen, be a good friend and go get us a snack. Perhaps some fruit juice," said Methuselah with a whistle, which is a parrot version of clearing his throat. "Now, if I may continue..."

Jen skipped away without a sound to retrieve snacks.

Sara was preoccupied as the whole thing had spooked her, but it was as if the parrot had read her mind.

"Things started getting really weird," continued Methuselah. "One day, Colonel Mike was away in another part of the complex. I was sitting in his office and going through reports when I heard typing in the next room. We kept an old typewriter there among cages, spare equipment, and boxes of paper. Someone was typing. The typist was typing very slowly--one key at a time."

"I put down a report on 'Fruit Fly Reproduction in Weightless Environments' (humans will study anything) and peeked in the room. What I saw surprised me more than anything I had seen since the yellow light hit me," said Methuselah. "There was a mouse on the keyboard banging one key after another with his feet. He was concentrating hard as he hopped between keys. He hadn't seen me, but there were a lot of words on the paper. Since I had never heard of a mouse writing a letter, I decided that it wasn't meant to be private. Since I'd learned quite a bit of Mouse-Speak over the years, I decided to speak up."

"What did you say?" asked Sara.

"I asked the little guy, 'What are you writing?'" said Methuselah. "Instead of running away or trying to hide, the mouse turned and looked at me. He said, 'I'm making a machine report of what I did since you humans seem to do it all the time.'"

"What?" asked Sara.

"Of course, I told him I wasn't a human," said Methuselah. "I told him, 'I am a bird.' I would have said 'Senegal Gray Parrot,' but Mouse-Speak is a very primitive language. It has no such precise words."

"'You speak excellent Mouse-Speak, for a bird,' he said. Then, I realized what all this meant!" said Methuselah. "'You saw it…. You saw the yellow light!' I told him."

"'I don't know what *yel-low* means,' replied the mouse. Mice cannot see color," explained Methuselah. "Then the mouse admitted, 'I did see a light. It was very big. It's all in the report.'"

"The mouse spoke with an attitude, as if he had been writing papers all of his life," said Methuselah. "I took this as an invitation and moved closer to the keyboard. This is what the mouse had written:"

MY TRIP UP HIGH IN THE AIR
AND THE BIG LIGHT

By Biff, Mouse, Number 34Z798J

Twenty days past I went up in the Rocket-Candle for a trip to the high air to be a Test Mouse for the Rocket Humans.

I wore a mouse-breathing suit and was kept from harm by rag straps and water bubbles. The loud rocket grated a little, but not like a car wheel and then the noise stopped.

I was very, very scared, but came to no harm and after a time I started to float. This was caused by being far from the ground and it made me stomach-less. I spit up greasy juice in my suit. I did not like this part, but the floating was good.

Then the big thing happened.

There was no window in my rocket to see out, but a very big light came through the wall and I went to sleep. When I awoke the rocket was floating down on something called a pear shoot and I was no longer the same mouse.

I was very smart now. I looked the same, but when the humans came to give me tests I learned more of their words each day.

Now I know almost everything they say. But since I cannot talk human speech, I decided to make this word report on the machine.

BIFF

Biff's Letter

"'This is very good for a first effort,' I told Biff the Mouse," Methuselah said.

"'First *ef-foot*?' Biff asked," said Methuselah.

"I explained to Biff that he was very lucky I saw his report instead of a human who didn't understand. They would think it was a practical joke," Methuselah explained.

"'Lucky?' Biff asked," said Methuselah. "I explained to Biff about how humans sometimes cut open things they don't understand to see how they work. Biff went pale and then ran back into his cage and closed the door. 'Are you going to tell them about me?' he asked in his small frightened voice."

"'No. You'll be safe,' I promised Biff," said Methuselah. "Then, taking the paper, I went to find Colonel Mike."

"Did Colonel Mike read the report?" asked Sara.

"That night, I told Colonel Mike about Biff," said Methuselah. "We decided right away to find out just how many other animals had been changed. Implications were clear. Aliens were still operating. Colonel Mike insisted that the Aliens had to be treated as enemies until we could find out who they were and why they were doing this."

"'But, why?' I asked Colonel Mike," said Methuselah. "'If everything they do to us animals has made us smarter and stronger?'"

"'Because these Aliens don't ask permission. They interfere in our world,' Colonel Mike explained. 'No one asked you if you wanted to be smarter,'" Methuselah recounted.

"'No one asked me if I wanted to be trapped and be a pet,' I replied, 'But you humans do that all the time. You make us your slaves and you do tests on us. You eat us. Need I go on?'"

Methuselah's questions challenged Colonel Mike.

"'Just as animals eat smaller animals, Methuselah,' explained Colonel Mike. 'You know about the food chain, and that is how things are. That is how things have developed on this planet. Now someone from another planet wants to change all that. Until we find out why, we have to assume these Aliens are just getting ready to eat us.'"

"'All of us? I asked,'" said Methuselah.

"Then Colonel Mike turned away," said Methuselah. "We were both upset. As it later turned out, he was right; the Aliens were out to devour us."

"What happened to Biff?" Sara asked.

"Colonel Mike brought Biff the Mouse home and replaced him with another one so the humans working in the laboratory wouldn't notice," replied Methuselah. "We started improving Biff's command of English. Unfortunately, with his mouse mouth, he could write and understand English, but couldn't speak well. So I had to translate anything he wanted said to Colonel Mike. An electric typewriter allowed him to write faster. Biff became quite a typist, dancing from one key to the next!"

"Meanwhile, we also checked the other animals," Methuselah explained. "Three other mice: Alpha, Beta, and George; three spider monkeys: Rollo, Suzee, and Joe; a squirrel monkey, Miss Baker; a chimpanzee, Caesar; and a dog, Professor Mutzie, had seen the yellow light. Apparently, not all animals had seen the 'Big Light!'"

"What did Colonel Mike do with all the smart animals?" Sara asked.

"Colonel Mike then began negotiating with the US Air Force for a real home for the animals that had served their country in space. At first, he got no support for a Zoonaut home," said Methuselah.

"Fortunately, the US Air Force was too busy with the war in Vietnam to supervise our lab. Whenever Colonel Mike wanted to take an animal for a night or weekend, no one objected," said Methuselah. "The sight of his car packed with monkeys, a dog, and a parrot was soon routine. Sentries started calling him 'Dr. Dolittle.' That would have been fine with Colonel Mike if we had been left in peace, but life was about to change."

SPACE MILESTONE TIME LINE – 1970S

- In **1971**, Salyut I, the first space station for Russia, went into orbit. The Mars 3 probe landed on Mars.
- In **1972**, Probe Pioneer 10 launched. It was the first human object to leave the solar system.
- In **1973**, American Skylab Space Station went into orbit...and stayed there until 1979.
- In **1975**, Russian Cosmonauts and American Astronauts carried out Apollo-Soyuz as the first Russian-US joint mission.
- In **1976**, the space probes Viking 1 and Viking 2 soft-landed on Mars and began sending back pictures.
- In **1977**, the long-distance probes, Voyager 1 and Voyager 2, were launched to study Jupiter and the outer planets. They carried messages of friendship, recordings of Earth sounds, and music to introduce us to any Aliens they encountered. Earlier, Pioneers 10 and 11 had small metal plaques identifying their origin for any spacefarers that might find them.
- In **1979**, Voyager 1 discovered a ring around Jupiter. The Skylab 1 space station fell back to Earth, landing in the Australian desert.

CHAPTER SEVEN

MAKING OUR WAY

"**B**y 1980, our dining room was like an Animal Grand Central Station with six typewriters on the table for anyone who wanted to communicate," said Methuselah. "Everyone did, except Professor Mutzie, a French Poodle, who was not adept at typing. The monkeys became very good at putting new sheets of paper in typewriters and clearing jammed keys. Someone usually was clacking away. After the invention of computers, this got much easier."

"Papers were piled high, and it was all General Mike (he had been promoted from colonel to general by now) could do to keep up. Soon he began missing meals and losing weight, so I had to speak up. One night, after dinner, General Mike, Professor Mutzie, and I were sitting on the back porch. I brought up the subject while the others were all inside watching *Wild Kingdom!* on TV," said Methuselah. "So, I asked, 'Boss, do you need help?'"

"General Mike looked at me and asked, 'What sort of help?'" said Methuselah. "'You're a general now, so shouldn't you have some lieutenants around to help?' I asked. He laughed."

"'How would I explain my dining room circus? Chimps lined up at the bathroom, and mice playing board games? You even do my taxes each year. You would all be in danger,' he said. 'No. No one else can help,'" Methuselah recalled.

"Professor Mutzie barked a long Dog-Talk sentence and I tilted my head to listen. It was simply brilliant and I told him so. He wagged his tail," said Methuselah.

"General Mike asked, 'What was that all about?' so I explained Professor Mutzie asked why don't we run an ad in the paper for an assistant—an animal behaviorist, civilian, and robotics expert ad,'" Methuselah said.

"General Mike was puzzled, so he asked me what good a robotics expert would do," said Methuselah. "Mutzie thought a robotics expert might design a talk-box for the animals to use."

"Wait a minute," Sara interrupted. "You mean you all talk? I mean, not just you, you're a parrot, but..."

"Yes," Methuselah replied.

"But other Zoonauts—cats, dogs, mice?" asked Sara.

"Gorillas, owls, and even orangutans! Yes," said Methuselah. "They do now. You've probably figured out you'll be meeting them soon!"

"And talk with them?" asked Sara, whose eyes were as big as saucers.

"Yes!" replied Methuselah.

"Wow!" said Sarah.

"I'd say that sums it up pretty well," Methuselah said with a laugh.

"But, how?" Sara asked.

"A 'voder circuit,' or mechanical voice box! It was Professor Mutzie's idea," said Methuselah. "He read every science magazine and was up on this stuff. I thought it might work from the start. It certainly would make things a lot easier for General Mike. I still remember that night."

"We sat thinking, almost like right now. We sat as the sun went down over the Everglades," said Methuselah. "Finally, he stirred from his chair and went to write the ad saying, 'Well, why not? The worst they can do is lock us up!'"

"General Mike wrote the ad, and I carried it like the report from Biff," said Methuselah. "I looked at the ad and studied it awhile. 'It's good, but why *philology*?' I asked."

"General Mike explained that philology was the study of languages since the new behavior expert would be dealing with many different animals," said Methuselah. "I asked why he included Pasadena, Texas, in the advertisement as a General Delivery address. He replied that he had just learned that Space Animal Research was moving to a new space center in Texas."

"So that is when you moved here?" said Sara.

"Precisely!" concluded Methuselah. "You are catching on!"

CLASSIFIED AD

WANTED FOR TOP SALARY

- **Animal behavior/veterinary/zoology expert t**o supervise special research animals for sensitive projects.
- Experience in psychology and philology helpful.
- Think differently and be changed by experience.

LIFETIME CAREER OPPORTUNITY!

Also seeking **expert in cybernetics/robotics**.

SEND RESUME TO:

McIntosh, General Delivery, Pasadena, Texas 77501

CHAPTER EIGHT

BEST FRIEND LOST

At that moment, Jen reappeared from the tunnel carrying a basket full of goodies – bottled fruit drinks for the two girls, fresh pineapple juice for Methuselah, and cheese and crackers for all.

They feasted.

"Now don't spoil your appetite," said Methuselah. "It's only a few hours to dinner."

"Don't be a Mom," said Jen. "I've got one already. She is enough."

Sara had a sad look on her face.

"Don't feel bad, Sara," added Jen. "I'm sure your Mom will return soon."

"Yeah," said Sara. "I guess. Did your Mom actually let you take all this food?"

"Sorta. I didn't ask. She was busy down at the clinic," said Jen. "Anyway, your Grandma cooks the greatest Mexican dishes. They are a lot better than this bland Army surplus stuff we get around here."

Methuselah threw his wing over his eyes.

"Miss Jen, do you mean to say that you absconded with these savory comestibles?" asked Methuselah.

"Not really, but I'm not quite sure that I know what you're saying," said Jen.

Methuselah began the serious interrogation.

"Did you take this food without asking first?" asked Methuselah.

"Well, maybe..." Jen confessed quietly.

"Terrific! I've become a bad influence," squawked Methuselah as he flapped about excitedly.

"No, you've just become a drama queen," said Jen.

Sara started giggling and soon they were all laughing uncontrollably.

"Methuselah has been telling me the wildest story about how you got all the animals to talk," said Sara, filling Jen in on what she had missed. "Is that really how you all came here to Texas?"

"Yes, we moved to Texas then, but not here exactly. General Mike managed to get us special quarters on the edge of the base where no one would bother us," said Methuselah. "For a while, people came around to see the animals. We watched them carefully to see if anyone was sympathetic enough to share our secret and if anyone was snooping."

"No on both counts. Everyone just ignored us. Things settled down," the old bird explained.

As the girls snacked on cheese, Methuselah told how the Stroud family arrived in Animalville.

"We had more help then," Methuselah said. "NASA assigned an administrator to the Animal Unit, Dr. Brooks Wagoner. He was a good man whose ancestors came from the same part of Africa, near Senegal, where I was born. General Mike let him in on our amazing secret because they had known each other for years. Dr. Brooks never seemed to get over it. He worried about everything: animals and Aliens. He worried that he didn't know the full story and that no one would tell him the full story. But mostly he worried about how to account for everything to the US Government in Washington, DC, without really telling anything. He kept talking about 'sitting on a time bomb.' Somehow, he came up with a little money each year to help keep the place running, but it was never enough. That is when we started marketing electronic toys and investing with the help of your father, Sara."

"What are you saying?" My father knew all about you?" asked Sara.

"Of course," said Methuselah, dropping the latest bombshell. "Mr. Abaroa was the genius behind Abaroatronics, and our breakthroughs in computer circuitry became the basis for our current financial success. We also launched some of the top electronic toys and video games on the market. You know, like RoboPuppy™ and Cyber-Evolution™!"

"I can't remember all the products," added Methuselah. "Mungo would remember, of course, since he works on all of the test versions."

"Mungo? Who is that?" Sara interjected.

"Another parrot," said Jen.

"Oh!" Sara replied.

"But the important thing is that it made us financially self-sufficient," Methuselah said. "I can't tell you how much!"

"Why not?" said Jen.

"Another secret to keep," Methuselah sighed.

Jen stuck out her tongue in response to Methuselah's disapproving glance.

"At any rate, for a while, we had a veterinarian, Dr. Marcuse, who had introduced your father's ideas to us, but he was killed in a car accident," said Methuselah. "Circumstances were mysterious, just like your father's recent accident, Sara."

"So you don't think it was an accident?" questioned Sara.

"I know it wasn't, Sara," said Methuselah. "They both knew too much about the secret success of Abaroatronics and its ties to Zoonauts and our investments. Jen, your father always blamed himself for Dr. Marcuse's death. I didn't know why until recently. We'll talk more about this later."

"In 1985, General Mike hired a young couple right from grad school," continued Methuselah. "Dr. Thomas and Dr. Angela Stroud were perfect. We all liked them. Later, another parrot, Mungo, became our Communications Chief, and I joined him on rounds with the Strouds to translate. I learned a lot. Tom and Angie Stroud (humans like nicknames) grew up in the same Iowa farm town. They were high school sweethearts and went to the university together."

Of course, Jen knew this story by heart.

"The Strouds married right after they graduated," said Methuselah. "They loved all of us animals, too, though at times, Tom has had second thoughts," said Methuselah. "'I studied animal behavior,' he would say, 'These aren't animals – they are little Aliens.' We laughed then, but we should have been more worried."

"Angie Stroud always wore long pants or long dresses because she had terrible scars on the backs of her legs. When she was twelve years old, lightening had hit the family barn," said Methuselah.

Jennifer winced.

"Angie had rescued all of the animals out of a burning building but was caught under the wreckage when it collapsed," said Methuselah. "Her father pulled her clear, but the scars never disappeared. When word of this got around, it touched the animals deeply, so we formed a pact where each animal swore to die before permitting any harm to Dr. Angie or Dr. Tom Stroud. That pact includes Jen and Cody and you, too, Sara!"

"Wow," Sara whispered.

Jen shrugged.

"My dear friend General Mike was getting pretty old, but he still made all the rounds himself, with me trailing along and translating," continued Methuselah. "It was a summer day in 1987. We were in the Primate House talking to Kongo, a young mountain gorilla, who joined Animalville after a shuttle flight."

"Kongo showed remarkable signs of intelligence and scientific ability," explained Methuselah. "We didn't know, just then, how far Kongo could go, but he had learned sign language well. He and General Mike were having a lively discussion about aerodynamic vectors, or something else I didn't fully understand. Dr. Tom was also a pilot, so when I heard sirens go off..."

"What happened?" asked Sara.

"I flew to the window and looked out. The sky was very dark. Then I saw a large tornado coming toward the base. I flew back to General Mike and Kongo. We all sprang into action. Kongo herded the other primates down into the cellar, while General Mike and I went to help Tom and Angie Stroud clear animals from the main lab that held the chimpanzees and monkeys. Kongo was the only gorilla back then. We all hurried down to the storm cellar and waited until the tornado had passed. It missed our labs, but when it was time to leave, we found General Mike unconscious on the floor."

"Oh my God!" said Sara.

"We raced him to the hospital. He had suffered a heart attack. Angie, Professor Mutzie the Dog, and I waited until we learned that he was going to be all right. Then Angie and Professor Mutzie went home. It was against the rules, but I turned the translations over to Mungo and sat up with General Mike in his hospital room all night. The next day, when he was feeling better, we talked about everything we had accomplished together from the moment Sergeant Otis Fox gave me to him right up to the tornado."

"Three nights later he told me, 'Methuselah, parrots live a very long time, but I think parrots exposed to the Alien's yellow light live even longer. You are my best friend and I'd guess I'm yours.' I nodded, unable to say anything," said Methuselah.

"'I probably will die before you. If that happens, you must promise me to go on and help care for the other animals,' said General Mike," Methuselah recalled.

"'I promise, General Mike' I said, 'but you're recovering. The doctors say you'll be okay,'" explained Methuselah.

"'Yes,' he said smiling. 'That's what they say.' He took a sip of water and then put down the glass and said: 'I'm feeling much better, and I'll be back at work before you know it,'" Methuselah recalled.

"'Well don't scare me like that,' I said. Then I told him, though maybe it was the wrong thing to say, 'An awful lot of us are counting on you!'" Methuselah said.

"He looked at me and smiled. He looked very tired. 'I know,' General Mike said."

Methuselah smiled.

"'It's always been my greatest pleasure and honor to have worked with you,' General Mike said. I felt immensely proud. Then he closed his eyes and went to sleep. I waited to make sure he was breathing okay and sleeping soundly. Then I sat down on the windowsill and slept myself," said Methuselah.

"I awoke to a loud shrill buzzing. Suddenly, the room was full of nurses and a doctor with something called a 'crash cart.' While they worked on General Mike, all I could do was stand and watch. Finally, the doctor said: 'He's gone!' Then he turned to me exactly as if I'd been a human and said, 'I'm sorry. His heart gave out,'" Methuselah said softly.

Methuselah paused for a moment. He was lost in thought as he remembered his old friend General Mike.

Sara reached out and stroked his feathers. The old bird went on talking, his voice sounded hoarse.

"They say birds can't cry, but I wailed and wept bitter tears," said Methuselah. "No one stopped me when I jumped down on the bed to kiss him good-bye. They covered him and took him out. I flew into the night alone. It was the worst moment of my life. I stayed in the woods for three days, which I had never done since I left Africa. I wailed, wept, and mourned. Then I remembered, thought, and finally slept. When I woke up, I knew General Mike was gone. There was an empty place in me that never has been filled to this day. Finally, I returned to the base. At Arlington Cemetery, I watched them fire rifles, fold a flag, and lower General Mike into the earth. I vowed then and there to do what I had promised – to take care of all the other Zoonauts as best I could."

SPACE MILESTONE TIME LINE – 1980s TO 1990s

- In **1980**, Voyager 1 and 2 flew by the planet Saturn and discovered two moons.

- In **1981**, Space Shuttle Columbia made its first flight, and in 1982, it made four more flights.

- In **1983**, Space Shuttle Challenger made three flights and a fourth in 1984. Sally K. Ride was America's first woman in space.

- In **1985**, the Space Shuttle Challenger blew apart seventy-three seconds after launch, killing six astronauts and Teacher S. Christa McAuliffe. This disaster almost ended the American space program.

- In **1986**, Mir (Peace) went into operation becoming the first permanently manned space station.

- In **1989**, Voyager 2 left our solar system to teach any extraterrestrials about us. NASA placed ambitious messages about our world on both Voyager 1 and 2. The Voyager greeting, recorded on a twelve-inch, gold-plated phonograph, contains sounds and images of Earth's life and cultures. A committee, chaired by Carl Sagan, picked the contents for NASA.

- In **1990**, Voyager 1 looked back from Deep Space and took the first photo of our Solar System. The Magellan spacecraft began mapping the surface of Venus using radar equipment. The Space Shuttle Discovery deployed the Hubble Telescope.
- In **1991**, the probe Galileo flew through the Asteroid Belt.
- In **1992**, The Space Shuttle Endeavor was launched on her maiden voyage. Mae Jemison became the first African-American woman in space.
- In **1993**, The Space Shuttle Endeavor made the first servicing mission of the Hubble Telescope.
- In **1994,** Sergei Krikalev became the first Russian cosmonaut to fly on a Space Shuttle.

Chapter Nine

THE STROUDS

"**B**ecause I had spent so much time with General Mike, I hadn't gotten to know Tom or Angie well," said Methuselah. "Now I was suddenly working with them every day."

"I kept busy, so I wouldn't think too much about missing General Mike. At moments, I still expected him to walk around the corner, smile, and say, 'Let's get to work!'" said Methuselah.

"It made me very sad. Angie Stroud noticed, but she said that this was normal. She told me that I would get over it. Eventually, I did recover from the loss, but I still missed General Mike. After all, I had known him for forty years. He would always be my best friend."

"There was a lot to do. Angie took care of the animals. We had many animals: gorillas, chimpanzees, monkeys, lemurs, dogs, cats, mice, toads, frogs, parrots, songbirds, owls, a raccoon, some snakes, and whole colonies of insects. Not all had been into space of course; those that hadn't were normal. Those who had been in space had three things in common--all of them were remarkable," said Methuselah.

"What three things?" asked Sara.

"First, we all became smarter," said Methuselah. "There was no way to tell how much smarter until we were tested. I have an IQ of 145. Mungo, a little green Senegal parrot who went into space in 1983, tested at an IQ of 152, but he has no dignity to go with it. The most amazing one is Kongo the Gorilla. Dr. Tom Stroud tested his IQ at close to 200. Kongo is so smart that he and Dr. Tom are working on some secret projects. One involves investing in the stock market – more about that later."

"The second thing was that we live longer, usually one and one-half times longer. This means I might see 2070 to really live up to my name!" exclaimed Methuselah. "Professor Mutzie the Dog was twenty-eight years old when he died. Biff the Mouse lived until he was twelve years old. Something the Aliens did made us much more efficient, smarter, and healthier."

"There was a third thing, and that was certainly very Alien," said Methuselah. "As all the animals started to mature into the period of life humans call puberty, they developed a special power. Some powers became obvious immediately. Ham the Chimpanzee could float and then he could levitate, but today he can fly. He was born just after General Mike died. Ham went into space two years later. Kongo's daughter, Patty Cake, can move herself and other things with her mind. That is called 'telekinesis' and 'psychokinesis.' Kongo, besides being very smart, learned how to 'step outside of time.' I know this sounds confusing, but it will become clear later. Mungo the Parrot is a natural linguist. He can grasp any language he hears and speak it immediately."

"Naturally, with these many strange and wonderful things happening, the Strouds decided these secrets had to remain truly secret," said Methuselah. "Only Dr. Brooks knows. He works in Washington, DC. That is where the government is located, and he worries enough for all of us. Of course, no secret can last forever, and now I guess it is finally out!"

"Now, as you know Sara, Tom and Angie Stroud had two children of their own—Jennifer, or 'Jen,' and Cody. No child has ever grown up with nursemaids like the Zoonauts to care for them. We taught them things no human has learned since Tarzan, who wasn't even real! You might wonder why I am telling you all this," Methuselah said. "Truth is, Sara, we need your help! Three things have happened – one good, one bad, and one that will launch us all on our greatest adventure. Now it is getting late, and you must go home. Don't tell anyone anything!"

Sara was visibly shaken as she came back to reality. She looked pale! She wondered if she had been dreaming.

Jen felt responsible but was at a loss for words.

"Well, life here in Animalville is always a surprise like that," Jen offered.

"I thought we were friends, Jen!" Sara babbled as she abruptly turned to go home. "How could you keep all this a secret from me?"

Secretly, Sara was glad to know something about Animalville and her father. She wanted to know more. What could Methuselah mean by saying they needed her help?

Then Sara turned around and smiled at Methuselah and Jen.

"See you tomorrow," Sara said.

"Why did you tell her so much!" asked Jen. Methuselah had confused her and she wanted an explanation.

"Jen, some things have been kept a secret even from you, but maybe I will let you know soon!" said Methuselah.

Then the old Senegalese Parrot flew down the secret tunnel for dinner. Jen followed after, under the watchful eye of Texas Bob, the monument to Animalville's past.

CHAPTER TEN

FABULOUS DISCOVERIES

Jen was unusually quiet at dinner that night. The tension between Jen and Cody was more than obvious. Methuselah knew he had to do something soon.

He flew into Jen's room while she pretended to do homework and started his conversation.

"Need any help?" asked Methuselah. "Egyptian history is one of my favorite subjects…they worshiped birds, you know."

"They also mummified them!" Jen retorted, looking up over the edge of her book.

"Yes, a nasty practice of the late Greco-Roman period started by the Greeks, as I recall," said Methuselah.

Jen was not amused.

"Don't get smart with me!" Jen said. "You know exactly what I'm thinking about. It was one thing for me to open my mouth, but why did you have to go and spill everything?"

"We don't have much time left before they return," said Methuselah in a lowered voice. "Things are happening faster since General Mike's death. I wish he could have seen these things, but…"

"You are babbling on as usual. What is your point?" Jen interrupted.

"I was just noting that many of you humans believe in a place called 'Heaven' where people go after they die, and they can look down and see how the rest of us here are doing," said Methuselah, noticing a feather out of place and adjusting it with great dignity. "I was simply reflecting. I don't know about this 'Heaven,' but I am certain General Mike would have been proud to see what we have accomplished –especially with 'The Mics.'"

"What have the 'Talking Jelly Beans' to do with anything?" Jen asked in hushed tones.

"Kongo and Tom had been working on the Universal Translator (UT) so animals could to speak to one another in English since it is the only language we all know," explained Methuselah. "We never found a suitable robotics expert; Mungo claims that the ones who applied were all 'dweebs' and that 'dweebs' talk too much."

"And you don't know anything about that?" Jen interjected sarcastically.

"Kongo began experimenting with computer circuitry and managed to design what you call 'jelly beans' – electronic modules – that many animals use to communicate. The correct term for these devices is 'mic' (short for microphone)," explained Methuselah, as if he hadn't noticed Jen's interruption.

"Using simple surgery, Dr. Angie Stroud implants this in the throat, and attaches the 'mic' to an animal's vocal chords. It can be placed in animals as small as a cat. Later, Kongo miniaturized it further for mice, toads, and even frogs. An animal recovers from surgery within days and then he or she can speak English as well as Dr. Tom or Dr. Angie. Mungo and I didn't need them of course, but the owls, Horace and Plato, got them. Then all the other animals wanted them, too. Soon, Dr. Angie implanted them as quickly as she and Dr. Tom and Kongo could churn them out. Communication became much easier, but we had to continually caution the animals to avoid those who might eavesdrop so they would not allow themselves to be overheard by other humans who might be listening."

"Exactly my point!" exclaimed Jen. "Why now? Why is it different now?"

"I am getting to that if you just let me fill you in on some details," said Methuselah.

Methuselah was clearly ruffled, but shook his feathers back into place.

"It was during this time that I began writing a history of Animalville. It told everything that had happened since I met Major Mike in 1944. Several other animals, including Horace and Plato, helped me. Soon, we were filling cabinets with reports, medical forms, test scores, and pictures of each animal that had come through the program since NASA had started. A special locked filing cabinet contains reports and essays written by animals themselves. If that were ever made public, our secret would be out, so we used two keys to unlock it. I have one and Dr. Tom has the other!"

"I'm still waiting…," said Jen sarcastically.

"Word of our abilities had already reached the wrong people," Methuselah continued. "The types of circuitry that we developed to go into the toys that Sara's father made were noticed. Some people saw the possibility of using this circuitry to build weapons, terrible weapons, of mass destruction that could do harm to millions of people. Well, that is not what Animalville is about! So we had to keep these secrets from falling into the wrong hands."

"Wait a minute!" said Jen. "Can't they just take apart the toys and figure out how the computer stuff works?"

"Good question. But, no." Methuselah shook his feathers. "It's not as simple as reverse engineering. We used techniques that could not be duplicated, but recently we've also started using materials that..."

"That what?" said Jen. She was getting excited in spite of her doubtful feelings.

Methuselah shrugged.

"There's no way to say this so that it doesn't sound dramatic, so I'll just say it," Methuselah said. "We are using materials and technologies that are not of this Earth."

Jen sat stunned for a moment.

"That. . . that. . .that means...," Jen stammered.

"Amador," said Methuselah. "May I go on?"

"OK, you've got my attention now!" exclaimed Jen.

"Good. Our labs are nice places with animals eating, chatting, and making new friends and discoveries," said Methuselah. "What you don't know, Jen, is that not all the animals here are happy!"

"What are you talking about?" asked Jen.

"Two in particular, Chuma the Chimpanzee, and Bandit the Raccoon, always caused trouble. They complained. They wanted changes. Then they wanted the changes reversed just to get their way. Worse, they were thieves! They stole from the other animals, from you and your family. While most animals don't collect things like humans, we all had a few gift keepsakes. Suzy the Orangutan had a favorite hairbrush. When she noticed it was missing, she told me. I already had heard complaints from several other animals, so Kongo and I went to see Chuma and Bandit. When we arrived, Chuma was sitting on his favorite seat, an old recliner chair, watching Bandit make a house of cards."

"'What do you two want?' Chuma asked crossly. Neither Chuma nor Bandit had yet received a mic, so the conversation was a mix of languages, all of which I spoke," said Methuselah. "Kongo demanded the return of Suzy's hairbrush, Horace's glasses, Mungo's autographed rockstar photograph, and all the other things that had been stolen."

"Chuma jumped up, ready for a fight, which would have been a mistake since Kongo is very strong, but Bandit the Raccoon waved his arms," said Methuselah. "'There is no call for that,' Bandit proclaimed, 'After all, we are all animals here, so it's not like we're humans.'"

"Bandit had said it without a smile, but it was plain that he meant to drive a wedge between the animals and the humans," said Methuselah. "Kongo was having none of it."

"'Humans are animals as well,' said Kongo. 'They just evolved differently. *If* we are to survive on this planet, we had best make our peace with them. Besides, there isn't a finer bunch of humans than the Strouds!'" Methuselah recalled.

"And General Mike," Methuselah said softly. "Even Chuma and Bandit lowered their eyes then. None of the animals would criticize General Mike. He had done too much for us; then Chuma just grunted and Bandit would not admit anything."

"'You have no proof we stole those things,' said Bandit, his long raccoon tail lashing furiously. 'What would we want with pictures, eyeglasses, photographs, and such junk? We have no use for them,'" said Methuselah.

"Kongo gave Bandit a fearsome stare," recounted Methuselah. "Then he said, 'I believe you took them just to cause trouble. I hate to say this, but Dr. Tom and Dr. Angie have to know.'"

"This was a serious threat, because it meant other animals would find out," explained Methuselah. "Chuma and Bandit glared and stood their ground. Kongo and I went to find Tom Stroud, who decided to talk to the two suspected thieves the next day."

"So what did they say?" asked Jen.

"When the next day came, Chuma and Bandit were gone. Somehow, they had escaped the base, but they left behind the items they had stolen all broken, torn, or otherwise ruined. They left a tiny note stating that they were going where they would be appreciated," said Methuselah.

"What we failed to notice at first was that a number of our experimental computer circuits were also missing, along with a large file of our government investments," he added.

"Where did they go?" asked Jen.

"Because the Space Center was on the edge of Houston—a big city—I wondered the same. Bandit could blend in well with the local raccoons, but Chuma was a chimpanzee. He'd be conspicuous. I was busy and soon forgot the entire business," Methuselah said. "My attention was focused on writing our history, which was about to become even stranger."

"Stranger?" Jen repeated. "What do you mean 'stranger?' I still don't understand why you are letting Sara know so much."

"In addition to Zoonauts' medical information, Kongo and I had compiled massive amounts of research data on both computer circuitry and the stock market. Since Sara's father was so important in developing what we know, she can help us fight them," stated Methuselah. "I am certain that Sara can help us in other ways, too!"

"But it doesn't make sense," asked Jen. "Why Sara?"

"Don't worry, I know what I am doing," said Methuselah. "It's all part of a plan."

Jen fell asleep without further worry because Methuselah's tone calmed her concern.

Sara's Grandmother Camille Flores hardly noticed that Sara had returned late from Animalville.

That night, Sara had a weird dream that Jen and Cody were lost in a swamp with a bunch of animals. Smelly monsters were chasing them all. They tried hiding out in a tavern, but nearly got caught.

Sara woke up in a cold sweat but couldn't remember much of her dream, except that the only way Jen survived was by one of the gorillas using some kind of mind control against the monsters.

At school the following day, Sara told Jen her entire dream, but neither knew at the time how useful that dream would turn out to be.

Sara's Scary Dream Foreshadows Future Events

SPACE MILESTONE TIME LINE – 1990S TO 2005

- In **1995,** Eileen Collins became the first female Shuttle pilot.
- In **1996**, The Galileo probe began transmitting data on Jupiter (December 1995).
- In **1997**, The Mars Pathfinder arrived on Mars and later began transmitting images.
- In **1998**, John Glenn became the oldest man in space.
- In **1999**, Eileen Collins became the first female Space Shuttle Commander.
- In **2000,** the US Near-Earth Asteroid Rendezvous (NEAR) Spacecraft began transmitting images of Eros.
- In **2001**, NEAR landed on the surface of EROS; American Dennis Tito became the first tourist in space after paying the Russian Space Program $20,000,000.
- In **2003**, the Space Shuttle Columbia broke apart on reentry into the Earth's atmosphere over Central Texas. NASA warned about contaminated debris. The Department of Homeland Security reported there was no sign of terrorism.

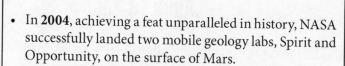

- In **2004**, achieving a feat unparalleled in history, NASA successfully landed two mobile geology labs, Spirit and Opportunity, on the surface of Mars.

- In **2005**, NASA's Earth-observing "eyes in the sky," included Earth-orbiting satellites, aircraft, and the International Space Station; these "eyes in the sky" provided detailed images of the flooding and devastation by Hurricanes Katrina and Rita. NASA worked to ensure the Department of Homeland Security and FEMA received the best information available to aid the rescue and recovery effort.

CHAPTER ELEVEN

BUSTED!

Methusaleh continued writing the Zoonauts' history on a carefully hidden, password-protected, computer file.

"As I told Jen, no secret lasts forever," said Methuselah. "Sara was certainly not the first outsider to learn about the Zoonauts. Remember Mr. Valentine and Mr. Christmas? General Mike and I were always worried the wrong government agents would find out about our secret. We worried we would be split up, studied, poked, prodded, or, maybe even cut open to see how we worked. As year after year passed and nothing happened, we started to feel safer at Animalville."

"In 1991, there was a war in a place called Iraq, so the US Government was busy waging that conflict. We went on writing our reports and teaching animals to talk through their mics. We gathered information about Aliens. It was a difficult task since we had never seen any Aliens then."

"Then one sunny fall day in 1992, everything changed. We never learned how the US Government agents found out about Animalville; that morning I happened to be looking out the window as trucks appeared. There were dozens: Humvees, ambulances, and even an armored car. They surrounded our lab and soldiers with guns emerged.

One man with a loudspeaker called for Dr. Tom Stroud to come out. Dr. Tom instructed me to keep the animals calm. Then he went out to talk to the soldiers. Meanwhile Kongo, Dr. Angie, and I rushed around to assure all the animals that everything would be 'alright.' We gave them instructions to avoid speaking in English."

When Dr. Tom Stroud returned, we noticed his face was white.

"'All the animals are being transferred,' Dr. Tom stated. 'I don't know what is going to happen, but we should all cooperate and everything will be fine,'" Methuselah retold.

Dr. Tom promised things would be OK.

"The trucks backed up to a loading dock, and each one of us was put into a sealed, darkened cage on the dock. I knew how afraid some of the animals were. We were all afraid we might be cut open and used for science or even eaten; however, everyone did as Kongo and I instructed. All remained calm. This was a good thing, because the humans were all armed with guns and looked very serious. I just concentrated on General Mike and the other good humans I had known. I hoped that there were good humans among the men who were now leading us into the cages."

"When the cages went dark, I thought about this for a while. Then, like many birds that are placed into darkness, I fell asleep. We were moved several times—at least I was because I didn't see any of the other animals. However, I heard Mungo singing a few times. They fed me— I don't know how long it was—perhaps even a day and a half. Finally they interviewed me," said Methuselah.

"Three men in white coats asked me many questions similar to the first conversation I had with General Mike a long time ago. I realized that they were testing my intelligence. Those questions were simple. Then one of them took a mic out of his pocket and put it on the table. For a terrible moment, I was afraid that they had cut open one of us to get it. Then I noticed it was incomplete and realized it must have come from the electronics bench where Kongo and Dr. Tom had built them."

"'What can you tell me about this?' asked the man in the white jacket."

"Well, it's some sort of electronic gizmo, I'd say," said Methuselah, with his head cocked to one side. "This is not my field, actually. My field is history, geography, and philosophy."

"'Methuselah, that's fine. Enough,' said the man with a thin smile. 'We know what it is!'" Methuselah explained.

"I didn't like his appearance," said Methuselah. "So I asked: 'Then why are you asking me?'"

"'We want to know who made this and how they learned to make it,' said the man with the thin smile," Methuselah said.

"'Whu-whu-well, I didn't do it,' I said," Methuselah reiterated. "I joked, using a funny voice to make them laugh."

"The other two agents laughed, but not the one with the thin smile. The man in the white coat with the thin smile glared at the other two and then at me. He plainly had no sense of humor," Methuselah said.

"'Very funny,' he said. 'Did Dr. Tom Stroud make this?' the man with the thin smile asked," said Methuselah.

"Dr. Tom Stroud is an animal behaviorist, not a...gizmo maker," said Methuselah.

"The men looked skeptical, doubtful, like they didn't believe me," said Methuselah.

"'What do you know about a company called Abaroatronics?' the men asked," said Methuselah, "I didn't answer them."

"'We know you have been making financial investments with these assets,' stated the man with the thin smile," Methuselah said.

"No, that was Kongo. Oops!" said Methuselah.

Methuselah was thrown off his guard for a moment. He had said far too much!

The thin-lipped man pressed him further with more questions.

"'We have plenty of evidence that Abaroatronics is using technology that is, at the very least, revolutionary. That technology originated in your research facility. It is a US government research facility. Now we want to know all about it,' the man with the thin lips demanded," said Methuselah.

Methuselah said nothing because he had little to say.

"'*If* you withhold information from a US Government inquiry you can be cited for contempt,' warned the thin-lipped man. 'That means it will be a very long time before you see any of your friends again,' he threatened," said Methuselah.

That did it.

Methuselah had enough.

"I'm saying nothing more," squawked Methuselah. "Get me a lawyer."

"'You can't have a lawyer! You are a bird!' said the thin-lipped man with a red face," Methuselah recalled.

"I have an IQ of 145," Methuselah bellowed. "If you hold me in contempt, then I deserve to be represented by counsel. Get me a lawyer!"

"The three men went into a huddle and began arguing among themselves. Finally, the mean one with the thin smile stomped out of the room," said Methuselah.

"Excitable, isn't he?" Methuselah asked.

"'Yes,' replied the other white-coated man. 'You can go back now. Thank you for your help,'" Methuselah explained. "He had a look of relief."

The two white-coated men escorted Methuselah back to the solitary cage where he grumped and complained until he fell asleep. He realized he and the other animals were in trouble, but he just didn't know how the animals were going to get out of it.

The answer came the next day when the covered cage was moved again.

An hour later, Methuselah was led into a room without windows and only two doors. Dr. Tom and Dr. Angie Stroud were already there. Dr. Brooks, Kongo, Mungo, Suzy the Orangutan, and two dogs, Emma and Belle, were also there.

"'What is happening?' I asked," Methuselah explained. "'Are the others safe? Where's our lawyer?'"

"Lawyer?" questioned Dr. Tom Stroud.

Methuselah explained to Dr. Tom Stroud about the three men and the one who had denied him counsel because he was a bird.

"They had no right to say those things," said Dr. Tom, shaking his head. "They were just trying to provoke you. The people we really have to convince are members of the Senate Subcommittee on Intelligence."

Methuselah knew about the Committee because he had discussed it with General Mike. The Subcommittee handled all of the spy stuff and secret programs for the US Government. Methuselah didn't realize that some of the animals were going to become spies as part of a secret program.

Methuselah surveyed the animals. Emma and Belle looked gloomy and resentful. Mungo was his usual cocky self. Suzy was looking around and taking in everything. Methuselah worried about Kongo, especially because of his confession. He looked stoic, that is, without expression, and thoughtful like a huge boulder. Methuselah knew from experience and the gleam in Kongo's eye that he was getting angry—a long, slow burn of anger that could erupt like a volcano.

Theoretical physicist, super-gizmo designer, financial specialist or not— Kongo was still a gorilla. Dr. Angie stood near him with her hand on his great hairy shoulder. She was whispering something to him and was probably asking him not to punch out the building wall. He was nodding with little bobs of his head, but his eyes were still red with rage.

Dr. Tom and Dr. Brooks Wagoner were talking quietly when the door opened and a man in a suit stuck his head into the room. He hadn't expected to see so many animals outside cages.

"Dr. Wagoner, you and your party may come in now," said the Ombudsman. An ombudsman is a government official appointed to investigate complaints against public officials.

The Zoonauts trooped into the room and found seats at a long table. At least Dr. Tom, Dr. Angie, and Dr. Brooks sat down. Suzy sprawled into a chair with her feet in her lap. The two dogs stood behind Kongo and Mungo.

Methuselah perched on the table across from the men in the suits. These were the senators who stood on the opposite side of the room. A uniformed policeman with a gun stood at each door.

"This is a senate hearing. Do we need to have armed guards?" asked Dr. Brooks as he cleared his throat and gestured toward the police.

"Yes, if you have these dangerous monkeys in here," stated an older senator as he waved a hand in the air.

"Senator, I am not a monkey," interrupted Kongo with a fearsome grunt. "I am a 300-pound gorilla. When angered, I can move fast enough to cross this courtroom in less than three seconds. You'll need bigger guns if you're going to treat us this way."

Kongo's voice was calm and controlled, but his anger just below the surface was evident.

The senators looked as if they just heard the most amazing thing in their lives. Perhaps they had. They stared with their mouths open until finally a younger member spoke up.

"Dr. Stroud, that's an amazing trick," exclaimed the senator. "How did you do it?"

Dr. Brooks responded with the first funny thing he had ever spoken.

"He didn't," said Dr. Brooks. "The parrot is a ventriloquist!"

Mungo laughed. Eventually, all the animals, Dr. Tom and Dr. Angie Stroud, and the senators with their security staff began laughing. As the laughter died away, Kongo spoke.

"I do believe that this is what is called 'breaking the ice,' or tension," said Kongo with a smile. "Senators, my name is Kongo."

The senators listened as the animals gave introductions and then each of the senators gave their names. These senators were powerful and could affect the animals in a major way. Methuselah had realized this from reading newspapers. The situation called for caution as the senators already knew some of the technological and investment activities of the animals.

The meeting lasted all day and all were careful throughout the interviews with each of the animals. There were questions about General Mike, our experiments, the mics that allowed Zoonauts to talk, Abaroatronics, the technology behind the new toys that were flooding the market, and their financial success. Though some Senators asked questions about Aliens, they never mentioned the "yellow light." Methuselah assumed they didn't know about it since he and General Mike had been careful to omit it in their reports. The senators and their staffs would have had to have read piles of papers written by other Zoonauts to uncover that secret.

Since it was getting late, the senators adjourned their meeting.

The senior senator agreed that the animals would return to Texas while the Intelligence Committee made its decisions.

Then they left.

The animals returned to their cages, but an odd thing happened. A young senator who had listened more than he spoke returned to say a few words to Dr. Brooks. After they talked, they shook hands. The senator smiled at the rest of the animals and left.

"Who was that?" Methuselah asked.

"That is the new vice president," said Dr. Wagoner. "He agreed to do all he could for us if we let him use our information about the toy circuits for the benefit of the country."

"You mean for the benefit of the military," said Kongo with a groan.

"Communications and medical monitoring, tracking hardware and software for ecological use, and for NASA," said Dr. Wagoner.

"I guess smart bombs and laser weapons could limit the number of civilian casualties if we ever went to war," said Kongo with a deep sigh as only the largest of gorillas can sigh. "Oh well, perhaps the senator will keep his word."

Kongo rubbed his throat where the mic was placed as he mused over the promise made by the new vice president. For the next eight years while he was in office, the vice president kept his promise and helped the Zoonauts more than the Strouds and the Zoonauts ever could have imagined.

Chapter Twelve

ANIMALVILLE, USA

The US Government can move fast when ordered. Animalville was all up and in place by the time the Zoonauts returned to Texas from Washington, DC. The location had been an abandoned amusement park south of Houston where lizards and tumbleweeds had taken over the forty acres of crumbling buildings and rides. It took a large group of carpenters and painters to clean it up when NASA acquired it for the Zoonauts in 1992.

The first half of the twentieth century in America, before there was television, was considered the Golden Age for traveling shows. Circuses, Wild West shows, and carnivals moved by wagons, trucks, and trains that crisscrossed the nation. In 1955, Disneyland opened and in its wake many large theme parks opened across the country. American families were suddenly jumping into cars, vans and station wagons to drive across brand new interstate highways to these huge parks where the families would ride the roller-coasters, buy souvenirs, and eat cotton candy from concessions in the parks.

Many of these theme parks closed since few were interested in touring shows. Others, like Texas Bob's Wild West Show, bought land and tried to survive as miniparks. Many failed, but Texas Bob hung on until the late 1970s, when he finally closed and moved to Florida to sell cars.

Even after the Zoonauts moved into the closed amusement park that had been Texas Bob's Wild West Show, the park looked like a fallen-down Texas ghost town. The fifteen-foot wood and plastic statue of Texas Bob towered at the edge of town near the old front gate. Wires for telephones, televisions, and Internet connections ran into the statue at Bob's head because that is where Mungo the Parrot decided to make his home at the Lucky Bravo installation.

The gorillas, chimpanzees, and other primates rebuilt the Funhouse Spook Ride into a series of pleasant apartments and workshops for their hobbies. The dogs occupied the Game Stalls and the Pond became the home of the secretive frogs and toads. The Merry-Go-Round became the place the animals gathered to discuss their problems. Texas Bob's Yee-Haw Barbecue became the Animalville Library. Luna and the other cats roamed the park and took shelter wherever they chose.

Methuselah wanted to name the place *IQ Zoo*, but Mungo's research showed that the name was already taken by some clowns in Hot Springs, Arkansas, where pigs pretend to drive cars. *Zoo IQ* was also not an option since the US Government wanted to keep the Zoonauts true nature "hush-hush." The name "Animalville" stuck.

Since the early years, a triple line of fencing, with warning signs and lights, sealed the boundary of Animalville. There is no gate. To enter Animalville, the Strouds and other human visitors had to fly in by helicopter, small plane (there is an airstrip), or travel through an underground tunnel and parking garage to a secret elevator that opened into the phony Texas Bob's Saloon.

Here, Drs. Tom and Angie Stroud maintain a fully-equipped veterinary hospital complete with a psychic research unit. There are also living quarters for the Stroud family. There are guest quarters for visitors though there are rarely any. A secret doesn't remain one for long if visitors are allowed to drop in. Usually the only guest was Dr. Brooks Wagoner.

The first night, after the Zoonauts moved in and looked over the place, they all met in Texas Bob's Saloon to learn the nature of their mission from Dr. Brooks. He told the most important things to the Zoonauts.

"The US Government is now convinced you are too valuable to be harmed or neglected," said Dr. Wagoner.

The Zoonauts all sighed together at once; they were relieved that no one was going to cut them open to see how they worked.

"The US Government is not yet convinced that Aliens are involved," said Dr. Wagoner. "That's hard for them to believe. Heck, it's hard for me to believe, but until we know differently, that is the course we are going to take."

"Keep watching the skies," Mungo croaked harshly.

Mungo had just discovered that he could imitate other voices, and he was practiced at the imitation of a cast of old movie characters.

Dr. Brooks raised an eyebrow and looked at him before he continued.

"Essentially, yes!" said Dr. Wagoner. "We must use all means to determine whether Aliens are visiting this planet, their intentions, and whether they have modified the Zoonauts. Now, as many know, General McIntosh, also known as General Mike, believed they were hostile."

Methuselah nodded as he recalled his conversation with General Mike.

"But none of us has seen an Alien," said Nikki the Golden Retriever. "How are we to recognize one if we meet one… him…her…uh…them?"

"Shoot first and ask questions later," drawled Mungo in his best cowboy imitation.

Kongo glared at Mungo.

"Enough, bird," rumbled Kongo.

Mungo subsided while watching him.

"Nikki has a point," said Kongo. "We've never seen an Alien; we have only experienced what Aliens do. We are the results of what they do. No human could do this to us. So I believe that we must carefully watch for other signs of Alien interference with animals. Eventually, they'll become impatient or careless, like this case in Australia."

"Exactly," said Dr. Brooks. "The Australians have not sent any animals into space, yet a koala was found at night in the Alice Springs Public Library reading books. He is very intelligent; as soon as Dr. Stroud finishes fitting him with a mic, we should have an answer to this puzzle.

Methuselah shook his feathers to get attention.

"Excuse me, Dr. Brooks," said Methuselah. "First, koalas are marsupials, not bears. Second, with a declining Russian space program, fewer animals go into space. Maybe Aliens are coming to Earth with their yellow light."

"Perhaps we will meet them then," added Mungo.

Suzy glared at Mungo for his interruption.

"Since you mention Russians," said Dr. Wagoner. "I will tell you that Russian Zoonauts will join Animalville soon. Please make them welcome and introduce them to our market economy."

It was Kongo's turn to ask a question.

"What about our investment plans, Dr. Wagoner?" Kongo asked.

"Yes, Kongo, you are to continue as before, but you must report all your findings directly to the vice president since that is an important part of our agreement," Dr. Wagoner concluded.

After the talk with Dr. Wagoner, the events at Animalville sped up. Two weeks later, the Russians arrived. There were three dogs, fourteen monkeys, two cats, and an assortment of frogs and insects.

Their leader, Laika, a Siberian husky, was named after one of the first Russian dogs that went into space in 1957.

Most of the Russian Zoonauts spoke English, and Laika was very fluent. The Russians were aware of the special abilities of their Zoonauts since 1987. With their shrinking space exploration budget under the new Russian economy, they decided to send their Zoonauts to the United States. The Russian Zoonauts were a welcome addition.

Laika and Kongo seemed drawn to each other as fellow leaders, thinkers, and finally, as friends. They spent much of their time together and discussed questions of how to learn more about the Aliens. Methuselah was the oldest Zoonaut, but had never considered himself the leader of the Zoonauts. He had served as General Mike's assistant and then became the Zoonaut historian. Kongo was left with the leadership role and was certainly the best choice. He worked closely with the Strouds and handled all the Zoonauts investments while he also generally watched out for all the Zoonauts.

There was an election in the United States about the same time the Zoonauts were celebrating their eighth anniversary of Animalville. The election greatly bothered both Kongo and Laika. If there were a new president, then there might be a new attitude about funds to support the Zoonauts at Animalville. Animalville still had plenty of money although Kongo had scaled back the toy chip program. Royalty payments and investments on Abaroatronics games were still arriving monthly. Animalville continued to safely make money in money market mutual funds from the investments and royalty payments.

The Zoonauts hoped after the election, NASA and Dr. Brooks Wagoner would remain in charge. Their worry was that the Zoonauts role might become more difficult with the new elected officials. Mungo aspired to become the "spin doctor" of public relations, and many of the Zoonauts agreed he was the bird for the job.

The Zoonauts were searching for someone to assist their mission when Jen's friend, Sara, showed up. Her abilities were exceptional, and the Zoonauts realized this.

While the Zoonauts continued to ponder the potential leadership changes and their impact on Animalville, Cough Drop, the Australian Koala, arrived. Four days after his arrival, he had his bandages removed from the operation to insert his mic. Kongo, Laika, and Methuselah visited him in the infirmary where he played checkers with Cody and Jen.

Somewhere, Jen had found a small Australian bush hat that fit Cough Drop. He wore it stylishly over one ear. Jen introduced Cough Drop to the Zoonauts. He looked at them with curiosity before he spoke.

"G'day," said Cough Drop. "Coo-eee, but you're a strange lot. You mean to tell me you've all been up in space?"

The Zoonauts nodded and Kongo smiled.

"Well, I was younger then and smaller," said Methuselah.

"I should hope so, mate!" Cough Drop chuckled. "I don't think any shuttle could get off the ground with a payload your size."

"Actually," Methuselah said, "I haven't been out in space. I saw the yellow light while I was very high up in a plane. But I understand that you had the experience on the ground."

"Too right, mate," Cough Drop said as he paused to move one of his checkers. "It happened to me out in the Never Never."

"I believe he means in the Outback," said Laika. "The great Australian Desert."

"Well, yeah, but not too far out," said Cough Drop. "It was near Coober Pedy. I was high up in a eucalyptus tree and staying away from humans and generally keeping simple. I've seen those koalas on the telly advertising Australian tourism and airlines. I don't have to tell you that it's not like that. I walked on the ground or climbed trees, drank water, ate eucalyptus leaves, and watched out for dingos and snakes. Boring, you might say, but a quiet life has its points. All in all, it seems a million years away now."

The Zoonauts listened as Cough Drop continued.

"One night, last summer, which is winter down in Oz, I was curled up in a treetop. I was keeping warm while pondering about where to find my next meal," said Cough Drop. "There was a light, I'll tell you mate, a bright light."

Kongo and Methuselah raised their eyebrows.

"The light came down through the clouds," said Cough Drop. "Humans ride in sky-lights, helicopters, and planes; at first I thought it was one of them. Then I got a creepy feeling. There was something that told me it was Alien. It acted funny and jinked around like it was lost or maybe confused. Then a really bright searchlight came out and swept around the sky until it hit me. My head hurt and I passed out. When I awoke, I wasn't alone."

"Who was there?" asked Methuselah.

"I was carried in a small cage between two strange creatures," said Cough Drop. "Like lizards, they were, but bigger. They were big as humans and walking upright. Each looked different, and they talked some ruddy gibberish. I realized they were taking me to their ship where there was a bright square with an open door."

"They walked me up a ramp and set me on a big metal table," said Cough Drop. I looked around and saw animals in cages against the walls. There was an iguana, a Joey, or kangaroo, as you call them, and a parrot. They fussed with an empty cage, and I realized then that cage was for me! I also realized I had become a lot smarter.

Cough Drop explained that he studied his cage.

"I studied my little flat cage, which looked like one in which you cook lobsters," said Cough Drop. "If I arched my back, I could pop it open. So that is what I did. When it banged open, the big lizards turned around and yelled. By then I was running for the door. Thank you, very much. One of them hit the door button, but I got out before it closed. Away, into the night, I ran. By the time they got the door open again, I was gone!"

Cough Drop sighed and removed his bush hat.

"I was in the dark, and suddenly I realized how smart I was. I also realized what a fix I was in," continued Cough Drop. "First, I wished I could save the other animals, not a koala-like thought. If I had tried to do that, though, they just would have caught me."

The Zoonauts winced.

"I wouldn't be here telling you this, either," said Cough Drop. "Yes, I was in the middle of nowhere with big lizards looking for me. I tell you, square, I didn't feel like a koala. I was as smart as a human. So, off I went looking for them. I thought the big lizards wouldn't follow me. Too, right! I looked back a few times."

"The Aliens cruised over the desert to hunt for me, no doubt. I followed a road to where I knew there was a road depot—what you call a truck stop. There was one near Coober Pedy where the long-haul trucks fill up. I figured if I could stow away on a big long haul that it would take me to a city. There, I could find some smart humans and learn what had happened to me."

"I was beginning to understand things in a new way," explained Cough Drop. "Human writing was a blur, but now letters were squiggly lines that I could tell apart! Reading became a great adventure that was frightening but exciting!"

The Zoonauts clapped to give Cough Drop his due applause.

"Thank you, mates," said Cough Drop. "I managed to climb behind the cab of a big sheep hauler and hid among the hoses where I slept there. When I awoke, we were out in the desert. I could smell sheep and hear their Sheep-Talk. Twice we stopped. I was getting hungry and thirsty but remained hidden. That night, we rolled into town, and I got off the sheep hauler. I found water, eucalyptus leaves, and slept a full day. Then I set out to learn about humans. For two weeks, I listened to humans talk and read. Luckily, I came upon an open basement window in a dark building. I crept in to look for food but found something more useful."

"What was that?" asked Kongo.

"I was in Alice Springs Public Library, so I began reading everything," said Cough Drop. "For two months, I crept in nightly to read. I read dictionaries and grammar books then maps; and histories. Finally, I read the science books. I was halfway through Charles Darwin's *Origin of the Species* when they caught me. I didn't have much trouble letting humans know that I was smarter than the average koala. Caught reading Darwin gave it away. I was sent to Animalville. I guess that makes me the first Australian in Animalville!"

The Zoonauts clapped for Cough Drop. Then they clapped again to offer him an encore.

"Thank you. Thank you, very much," Cough Drop said. He took a bow, and with a smile of relief, he placed his bush hat back on his head.

Drs. Tom and Angie Stroud with Cough Drop
Ham, Laika, Methuselah, Jen, and Cody.

Chapter Thirteen

METHUSELAH AND GENERAL MCINTOSH, SUPERSPIES

Methuselah was about to share his greatest spy adventure with Jen and Sarah.

"Remember what I told you about Mungo?" Methuselah asked. "He was fascinated with voices, television, the Internet, and anything else involving communication. He was probably the first creature at Animalville to learn of the tragic events of September 11th."

"How?" asked Sara.

"He lived in the great plastic and wood head of the Texas Bob Statue," explained Methuselah. "He surrounded himself there with televisions, computer screens, keyboards, radios, phones, and all manner of electronic gear. Sometimes I worried that all this electricity was frying his little bird brain."

"Did you fly with him often?" asked Jen.

"Three times a week on the orders of Dr. Angie Stroud. Mungo had to spend an hour exercising his wings flying around Animalville, which I did with him, partly to make sure he did it, and partly because I liked him," said Methuselah. "Then one fine spring day in 2002, after we had made two circuits in the park and were resting at the old water tower, Mungo said something I thought was very strange."

"I picked up a report on Radio India, in Hindi, about two pandas that had come out of the Himalayan foothills and were living at a monastery," said Mungo.

"The monks there consult with them often for their wisdom," said Methuselah. "So are you asking me if I think it is a hoax or something dreamed up by the humans to get attention?"

"Yes," replied Mungo. "Do you think there could be more animals the Aliens changed?"

"I don't know since I never heard of pandas going into space, but let's call the India Government and ask them to ship the pandas to us," said Methuselah.

"These pandas aren't in India," said Mungo. "They are in Tibet. The India Government heard of the pandas, but no one has seen them."

After a brief moment, Methuselah replied.

"We should go report this to Dr. Tom," said Methuselah.

Dr. Tom called Dr. Brooks in Washington, DC. After a few days, we got the information we were anticipating. The pandas were in a monastery near the town of Rima. So far, the Chinese Government had not done anything about them.

"Maybe they don't believe it," said Mungo. "Yet..."

"Well, when the Chinese find out perhaps they'll send us the pandas," said Methuselah. "The Australians sent us Cough Drop."

"The Australians have been our friends for many years," Mungo said. "The Chinese are suspicious of the United States. They won't send the pandas here."

Methuselah thought for a moment. The Chinese had opposed us in Korea. They still had a Communist Government. This was all human politics and something that he had never fully understood. But Methuselah knew one thing: an Alien invasion was much more important than politics.

"Then we must go get them," said Methuselah.

Mungo and Dr. Tom looked strangely at the old Senegalese Parrot.

As the four of them (Mungo, Dr. Tom, Methuselah, and Laika) boarded the plane for the town of Rima to rescue the pandas, Methuselah realized he had said something aloud that he should have kept to himself. The four flew from Animalville to Hawaii then on to Australia and then to India. They landed at the Sadiya India Air Force Base.

For Methuselah, it was strange to return to India and the Himalayas again since he had not been there since World War II. He gazed out the window of the US Air Force jet to see the Himalayas shining in the sun. Mount Everest was hundreds of miles away but still looked gigantic as they passed the mountain peak.

"I understand why Kongo could not come," Methuselah said to Dr. Tom.

Mungo was sleeping.

"There are no gorillas in India, and I know we need Mungo because he speaks all Chinese dialects," said Methuselah. "But why did we bring Laika?"

"Laika is very wise," explained Dr. Tom. "Laika also understands some Chinese and he's a dog. Dogs are everywhere and no one will notice him."

"Mungo and I, we are African parrots," Methuselah stated. "Won't someone notice us?"

"Most people will just see two birds," said Dr. Tom. "Only a bird-watcher would know the difference. Hopefully, you won't be in Tibet long enough to be discovered."

"Ummm," Methuselah mulled over the statement in his head for a bit and then posed the question that was bothering him.

"And me? Why me?" asked Methuselah.

"Mungo is a smart bird, but he is not wise," said Dr. Tom. "He also talks too much. Laika is wise, but he is a dog. Dogs are common and the monks at the monastery may not respect him. However, you have both wisdom and age; you will speak for Animalville as our best spokesman—'spokes-being,'" Dr. Tom said, correcting himself. "But there is one other thing."

"Yes?" Methuselah nodded almost falling off his perch.

"This mission is likely to be dangerous. If you can't get the pandas out safely, don't risk being captured," cautioned Dr. Tom. "You must make that decision. If it looks too dangerous, then the four of you must get away and back to the border into Burma."

"I'll bring them home safely," Methuselah promised. He hoped he could rise to the challenge.

Just then Laika joined the three Zoonauts.

"I heard a thud in the baggage area," said Laika. "I am going back there to investigate."

"All right, Laika," Dr. Tom said. "Be careful."

"I am going to go along as backup," said Methuselah.

To the amazement of both Laika and Methuselah, they found a young stowaway aboard.

Cody Stroud!

"Excuse me, young man," questioned Methuselah. "What exactly do you think you are doing here?"

"Please don't turn me in," Cody pleaded. "I just had to come along! I can be very useful."

"No, you won't," Laika growled. "You can stay right here in the plane until we fly home."

Cody was clearly frightened by Laika, but Methuselah just knew Cody would get into even more trouble if he was unsupervised, so he quickly devised a plan.

"Laika," Methuselah improvised, "I'm sure Cody can be useful in this mission. Let's keep his presence here a secret between us."

Laika wasn't sure but finally agreed.

A truck was waiting for the Zoonauts and Dr. Tom at the airport. Mungo, Laika, and Methuselah got in the back while Dr. Tom rode up front with a soldier who drove them to a point where Dr. Tom could study the border. Cody remained hidden in the supply bag.

The governments of India and China disagreed about where the borders should be located. Each wanted more of the other's territory,

There were watchtowers, too! The road from Sadiya to Rima passed through a checkpoint where armed Chinese guards inspected all those coming from India. Armed India troops did the same for those traveling from China, although there wasn't much traffic. Mostly the guards stood around and glared at one another.

"Well," said Mungo, "Methuselah and I can fly over a fence, but what about Laika? He can't."

"You must fly east along the fence and Methuselah must fly west. When you find a break where Laika can get safely through, then return. We'll use the closest one," said Dr. Tom.

As it happened, Methuselah found a place where the wire did not completely cover a ravine only three yards to the west. At dusk, Mungo and Methuselah flew across the border to a rock formation that looked like a crouching bear. They waited there while Laika crept under the wire and joined the two an hour later. Laika arrived dragging the provisions bag with Cody secretly inside it. They slept there until dawn.

When the sun rose, they made their way along the road to Rima. At last, they saw the town to the right. To the left, up the hillside, stood a tall stone monastery where the monks were holding the pandas. It was a short trip to the monastery. First, Methuselah decided that Mungo and he should go scout out the town to work out a plan.

There was a busy market in Rima, and there were religious Buddhist pilgrims coming through to visit the monastery. There were also Chinese flags and soldiers, but they didn't seem to be particularly excited about anything. All in all, it was a case of humans just going about their business. That was fine for the Zoonauts. They flew back to the hiding place.

"Cody," said Methuselah. "Use the supply bag and make a crude tunic; then roll in the dust so you look worn from travel."

"Cool...but why?" asked Cody.

"You and Laika are going to become Buddhist pilgrims," said Methuselah. "Are you ready?"

"Sure, but what do I have to do?" Cody asked.

"Join one of the groups entering the monastery," explained Methuselah.

The Zoonauts were in luck. A group of pilgrims just arrived at the monastery. They were busy spinning their prayer wheels by the wall. Cody had just enough time to put together his poor robes. He was quite funny to watch as he tried his best to make himself look like a Buddhist pilgrim.

"You had better let me do the talking," said Laika. "You don't know any Chinese."

"And you don't think they'll notice a talking dog?" Cody retorted.

"Don't argue with me," said Laika. "If it were my decision, you would still be hiding in the plane."

"All right, but once we're inside, follow me. After all, you are 'just' a dog."

The pilgrims were too busy with meditations to notice the young boy and his dog join them. Then a monk unlocked the door and let them all in. Mungo and Methuselah watched Laika and Cody slip in with the group. The two birds flew over the wall to meet them. Together, they started searching for the pandas, but somehow Cody got lost in the crowd of pilgrims. They eventually found the pandas in a main hall of the monastery and crept in to listen to the monks.

The pandas sat on cushions surrounded by a small circle of monks who listened as the head monk asked the two pandas questions. This leader wore a banana-shaped hat on his head. It was really an indication of rank, like a bishop's miter or headdress.

Methuselah could not follow much of it, but Mungo translated and interspersed his own comments such as: "Good answer!", "Well said!", and "They are very wise." The discussion seemed to be about the place of humans and animals in the world. The pandas thought about what they would say before each answer; both were always polite and courteous.

Laika and Mungo stand guard while Hsing-Hsing and Ling-Ling reveal their extraordinary powers and wisdom to the monks in the monastery.

They could not exactly 'speak,' but had learned a form of sign language and grunts that the head monk seemed to understand. When they weren't 'speaking,' the pandas reclined on pillows and munched on bamboo shoots.

Methuselah was just thinking about how to approach the pandas when a young monk spotted the Zoonauts. He approached them while waiving a broom to shoo the Zoonauts away.

"*Ni dui ke ren shi fen bu li mao*," said Laika in Chinese. In English this translated to the phrase, "Are you so impolite to all your guests?"

The monk screamed and ran toward the other monks. He yelled in Chinese.

Chaos ensued.

"What is he saying?" Methuselah asked Mungo in a hushed whisper.

"*Dong wu hui shuo hua la!*" replied Mungo.

"I mean, what does it *mean* in English?" demanded Methuselah.

"More talking animals! That's all," replied Mungo.

The monk's attention, along with the pandas, shifted to the Zoonauts.

"Follow me," said Methuselah as he hopped to the floor and walked forward. Laika followed behind with Mungo perched on his back.

"*Ne hao*" (hello), said Methuselah in Chinese while he nodded in an attempt to appear impressive and regal, which parrots typically do not look when they are walking rather than flying.

The monks backed away to give the Zoonauts a clear path.

Finally, the Zoonauts stood face-to-face with the two pandas.

The Zoonauts bowed while the head monk with the banana-shaped headpiece attended them.

"Greetings," said Methuselah. "I am Methuselah. I am here as a representative of Animalville where the talking animals have gathered."

Methuselah waited for Mungo to catch up with his translation into Tibetan and Chinese.

"*Ne hao, wo shu Methuselah,*" translated Mungo. "*Wo shu dong wu dai biao.*"

The first question was easy.

"*Ni chi fan la ma?*" asked the monk. ("Have you eaten yet?"—A typical Chinese greeting.)

"*Chi la,*" replied Mungo. "*Ni, na?*" ("Yes, I have eaten. Have you?")

Dr. Tom had said to keep it simple, but the monk's next question was a problem.

"*Ni lai zi shang tian ma?*" the monk asked. This meant, "Are you from the Gods of the Sky?"

Dr. Tom and Methuselah had talked about lying. Methuselah was not prone to lie, yet remembered Dr. Tom's advice. He had said that the most important thing was to protect Animalville.

If Methuselah had to make something up to do that, well, that is what spies do.

Up until that moment, Methuselah had not thought of himself as a spy. He knew about spies. He also knew that a captured spy was usually shot. He carefully pondered the monk's question before answering.

"The Sky Beings give us our powers, yes," said Methuselah to the monk.

"Yes. All animals are brothers under the sky," said the monk.

There was more excited talking. In the commotion, Methuselah noticed one of the pandas signing something to Mungo.

"What's he saying?" Methuselah asked.

"He's saying: 'You're doing fine. Keep it mystical,'" Mungo translated.

Methuselah did. He told how many animals had received mystical powers and how they were charged with the responsibility of saving Earth. He explained how the animals had gathered in a secret town and that they needed the pandas to come with them since their wisdom would be appreciated. The monks listened carefully. While they clearly were in awe of the Zoonauts, it was also obvious that they didn't want to give up their pandas. The old monk looked unhappy.

As the monks talked, Methuselah learned more through Mungo's translations. The pandas were named Hsing-Hsing and Ling-Ling. They were a mated pair, which meant they had been living as a couple in the forest until the night the bright light hit them. They awakened before the Aliens could capture them and fled westward until they came to the monastery. The monks were very good to them, but the head monk did not want them to leave. They were virtual prisoners until the Zoonauts' arrival.

Now there was a good chance the monks would keep the Zoonauts, too.

"I wondered about that," said Laika, who watched the two monks closing grills over the windows so perhaps Methuselah and Mungo could not fly out.

"I thought they would consider us spies, not captives," replied Methuselah.

At that moment, when Methuselah had figured his long, strange career was about to end, another monk ran in toward the Zoonauts gathered with the monks.

It was Cody! He had traded his ragged sack tunic for a monastic robe. Clearly he was a master of disguise!

"Quick, we must do something!" Cody whispered to Laika. "Some army trucks are heading this way. I just spotted them from the top of the roof!"

The Zoonauts didn't have much time to question what Cody had been doing on the roof, or how he got his new clothes.

"What, please, did this novice just tell you?" asked Hsing-Hsing.

"He has seen a great vision that you must leave with us immediately," said Laika.

"Kuai fai kan!" ("Look!"), shouted Cody in flawless Chinese.

Everyone ran to the windows. Methuselah flew over and perched where he could see out. Three large, green trucks were coming up the road toward the monastery.

The monks all started yelling.

"Chinese soldiers," yelled Mungo over the din. "They are coming to take the pandas away!"

At that moment, the head monk pulled back a curtain to reveal a dark opening to a hidden passage. He motioned the Zoonauts toward it. Hsing-Hsing, Ling-Ling, Cody, and Laika ran toward the dark passage. As they reached the exit, they heard a distant pounding as Chinese soldiers broke down the door.

The head monk turned to us then and spoke in almost perfect English.

"'You must go and take the pandas with you!' he said."

"You speak English?" Methuselah asked.

"Yes," said the monk. "I worked with the US Air Force during the war."

"So did I," replied Methuselah with a bow. "Thank you, very much."

Methuselah turned and then hurried after Ling-Ling down the dark passage, which turned out to be a stairway that went down a very long way.

The passage stairway led the Zoonauts and pandas to a cave. There, the Zoonauts and pandas waited until the sun set over the Himalayas. Then, with Laika in the lead, they all made their way back to the ravine where Laika dug and crawled under the wire.

Methuselah realized he hadn't taken into account that the opening that was big enough for Laika and Cody to slip under was much too small for the pandas.

It was a confusing moment as all the Zoonauts looked at each other until Laika spoke up.

"Well, I'm still a dog," Laika said.

Then Laika began to dig under the wire to make the hole larger. As he dug, the pandas pushed away the dirt so it would not clog up the hole. The pandas were not well-suited for moving earth, but they worked steadily, with Mungo and Methuselah perched where they could watch out for trouble. It wasn't long before Methuselah and Mungo found it.

First, Methuselah saw the lights of vehicles coming down the border. Then Mungo heard the blowing of whistles and orders shouted in Chinese.

"They're coming to search the fenceline for the pandas," Mungo cried out. "We must do something."

"In case you didn't notice, I am not MI6," Methuselah said crossly.

"No, but you read everything," said Mungo. "Do the Chinese believe in ghosts?"

"Yes," Methuselah replied. "Yes, they do!"

"Good," said Mungo. "Here's the plan..."

As the Chinese soldiers came down the fence toward the Zoonauts, their officer suddenly screamed at them and called them back. He gave orders to them to return to their trucks. This, of course, was a credit due to Mungo.

Mungo had flown down to the border crossing and had listened to the officer long enough to learn how he spoke. It wasn't hard for Mungo, who is a perfect mimic, to create some confusion. He imitated the Chinese officer, and the Chinese soldiers turned around and left. However, it wasn't long before they returned.

When the Chinese soldiers returned, their officer was with them. He cursed and threatened them as they advanced toward the Zoonauts. Mungo and Methuselah were ready and hid in the darkness where they began to make eerie sounds. Methuselah had no idea what a Chinese ghost might say.

"Whooo-ooo!" cooed Methuselah eerily in the hope his ghost imitation would scare away the Chinese soldiers.

It did! The soldiers stopped and chattered wildly.

Zhan shy! Gan sha de?" ("Stop! What are you doing here?") wailed Mungo in Chinese with a spooky reply.

The Chinese soldiers were all talking at once while their officer yelled at them above the racket.

"They say I am a ghost of the mountain," said Mungo proudly.

"Well, don't disappoint them," Methuselah said. "Give them a story to take home!"

Mungo puffed himself up and bellowed.

"Wo shi shan yao. Gun Kai! King! King! King! Kong! King! Kong!" ("I am the Ghost of the Mountain. Leave this place! Now!") Mungo said.

The Zoonauts rattled the metal fence while Mungo added a flood of Chinese words. The Chinese soldiers broke away with screams. They fled with their officer firing into the air to stop their retreat. They ignored him and soon disappeared into the darkness.

Mungo and Methuselah hurried to the opening in the wire fence where Hsing-Hsing and Ling-Ling were just squeezing through as they did not want to see if the Chinese soldiers would return.

"I heard shooting," said Laika. "Was there trouble?"

"Oh, no," chirped Mungo. "It was fun."

For once, Methuselah agreed with the little bird.

"Cody, where did you learn Chinese?" Methuselah asked.

"Oh, I've been taking lessons from Mungo," replied Cody.

"I should have guessed," said Methuselah.

Three hours later, the Zoonauts were all aboard the US Air Force jet and heading for home. On the way, Laika tried to teach the pandas to say, "Hello, Mr. President," but they were very confused.

"Hei gou, plan za-da bus hi?" the pandas asked.

To the pandas, it sounded like Laika was speaking in the manner the Japanese soldiers tried to speak Chinese.

Laika tried to convince the pandas the phrase was a polite one, but they refused to believe him or repeat the phrase because they interpreted its meaning differently.

The Zoonauts all roared with laughter when the pandas finally explained the meaning of the phrase and translated its meaning from Chinese to English: "Are you a cheating dog?"

They would never say that to Laika!

CHAPTER FOURTEEN
ALIENS REVEALED

When the Zoonauts finally arrived back at Animalville, the team felt like celebrities. Laika accompanied Hsing-Hsing and Ling-Ling to meet the new President.

Methuselah was ready for a good bird bath and a long nap! After resting for a few days, he went to see Mungo in the Command Center in Texas Bob's statue's head. As usual, he was typing away on a keyboard while watching three video screens.

"You'll go blind one of these days, you know that?" Methuselah said.

"Ha-ha-ha!" laughed Mungo.

"I've been telling him that, but he won't believe me," said Luna, a long, lean, gray cat who arrived with Laika and the other Russians.

Luna was fascinated with Mungo. She was trying to understand his obsession with technology. She liked to tease him about it.

"Mungo, does it bother you that Luna teases you?" Methuselah asked.

"Bothered? By Luna?" Mungo replied. "No, she is my biggest fan. Someday, when I am running the *Tonight Show*, I'll make her my announcer."

Luna curled up on a large speaker and watched Mungo surf the Internet. She favored Methuselah with a cat smile that any bird would find disturbing, except Mungo. Then she ghosted away and walked through a wall.

That is Luna's power. She can 'ghost' through solid objects, walls, and such. Not even a smile remains.

"Silly cat!" said Methuselah, who shook his head. "Mungo, did you call me?"

"Yes. On the news this morning there was a story from China," said Mungo. "The Chinese Government is blaming India for the theft of the two pandas. The India Government has no idea what they are talking about."

"Oh, dear," Methuselah replied. "I hope we didn't start a war!"

"I don't think so," Mungo laughed. "The head monk at the monastery gave an interview to a French reporter. He told the French reporter the pandas weren't pandas at all, but rather space creatures, and they've gone back to space! The Chinese are going to look pretty silly if they keep this up after all that!"

"That's why I came to see you," said Methuselah. "Hsing-Hsing and Ling-Ling have started talking. I thought you would like to be there!"

The two flew to Texas Bob's Ye-Haw Barbecue where many animals had gathered with the Strouds and Dr. Brooks. Mungo and Methuselah found a perch in the rafters near the owls, Horace and Plato. Later, they decided to join Jen and Cody. Hsing-Hsing and Ling-Ling were sitting between the Strouds. Their throats were without bandages. Each had a tall glass of lemonade to soothe their throats, which were sore from the operations. Dr. Stroud had only gone through their mouths to implant their mics. As Mungo and Methuselah flew in, Kongo rose to his feet.

"Order. Order. My friends, we have great and grave news," said Kongo.

Kongo leaned forward on his knuckles and cleared his throat with a sound that Mungo compared to an avalanche.

"We now know where the Aliens come from and what they want!" Kongo said.

There was a sudden racket as everyone began talking at once, but Kongo raised a huge hand, and the noise subsided. Besides his leadership role, Kongo had the respect of all the Zoonauts because of his size since he is a large and powerful gorilla.

"The same yellow light that we saw has changed our two newest members," said Kongo. "Hsing-Hsing and Ling-Ling, while in their bamboo forest in southern China, received their powers! While no one knows what Ling-Ling's power is quite yet, Hsing-Hsing's power is both important and amazing. He will tell us more."

The Zoonauts have superpowers like the ability to fly or turn invisible. Some powers affect objects, like the power that an animal uses to move or bend objects. Some powers are like Luna's gift to ghost through walls. Some superpowers involve mental feats, such as Mungo's ability with language or Methuselah's memory. Other superpowers involve perception, such as Nikki the Golden Retriever who hears at great distances. A few superpowers involve altering reality, like when Laika projects a defensive shield, or Kongo briefly stops time. But Hsing-Hsing's superpower brought us the most direct knowledge of the Aliens themselves.

Hsing Hsing took a sip of lemonade and looked at the Zoonauts gathered in the room. When he spoke, his accent was still heavy Chinese, but he was learning English fast, perhaps as fast as Mungo.

"My friends, I must greet you and thank you for bringing my mate Ling-Ling and me to your fine country," said Hsing-Hsing. "The last few weeks are very confusing for us. So much, many new things sit in our heads. It is almost not possible to speak of them. A new land, a new speaking of language…"

Ling-Ling leaned in close to Hsing-Hsing and whispered something. Hsing-Hsing smiled.

"A new…learning a new language, yes, and a thing which you call power," said Hsing-Hsing. He looked at Dr. Tom Stroud who nodded. "I will let Dr. Thomas Stroud tell you of it. His words are better than mine."

Dr. Tom stood up and every furry, feathered, or scaled head in the place focused on him.

"We know that when Hsing-Hsing and Ling-Ling came to consciousness in the forest after seeing the yellow light that they were alone," said Dr. Tom. "There were no Aliens there; they had the presence of mind to immediately leave the area. They traveled west and ended up at the Rima monastery where Mungo, Methuselah, and Laika found them and helped them escape."

Hsing-Hsing nodded to Methuselah with a smile.

Methuselah felt immensely proud sitting on Cody's shoulder.

"How about that?" asked Cody. He winked and tapped Methuselah on the wing. "You're a hero now."

"I never get to do anything!" sighed Cody in his next breath.

"Don't start," whispered Methuselah. "You're just lucky I didn't tell anyone about your prank, young man!"

"Shhh!" said Jen from nearby.

Dr. Tom continued.

"We believe that this time the Aliens actually touched the pandas because of the power they have," said Dr. Tom. "Why did the Aliens leave without them? Well, perhaps the pandas were too large, or the Aliens learned something that scared them. At any rate, before the Aliens left, Hsing-Hsing absorbed their memories. So we now know who the Aliens are and where they come from and what they want."

The hall was so quiet that you could hear a pin drop.

"Their dark planet swings in the same orbit behind Alpha Centauri," said Dr. Tom.

"This means it is not visible from Earth, though human astronomers have long suspected its presence," Cody whispered in Methuselah's ear. This was a fact he may have picked up in his science class, but more than likely from Kongo.

"Amador is rich in minerals, but poor in everything else like breathable air and drinkable water," said Dr. Tom. "The best parts look like a slum in hell. Volcanoes, fire pits, lava flows, and other charming features dot the landscape there. Great factories turn out large menacing machines. Occasionally, a mountain blows up or an island sinks into the alkaline seas. The worst fact is the Amadorians themselves. They might have conquered the universe long ago if they had been more numerous, but they have a low birth rate."

Cody just couldn't resist another comment.

"Methuselah, would you like to have been born on Amador?" asked Cody.

Methuselah remained silent while Jen just stared at Cody with her beady eyes.

"At present, there are only a few thousand of them," said Dr. Tom. "The average Amadorian is awesomely creepy, and you have seen them before."

"What do you mean, we have seen them before?" asked Kongo, whose attention was suddenly focused on Dr. Tom's last statement.

"Amadorians come in all shapes and sizes. No two are alike," said Dr. Tom. "They look like every possible variety and design of what we on Earth call a 'dragon'—those creatures of myth and legend that never really existed. Or did they?"

"Do they really exist?" asked Jen. "If so, how did they get here so long ago?"

"At least a thousand years ago, a group of thirty or forty Amadorians decided to stop fighting each other and cooperate. They built a junky spaceship," said Dr. Tom. "They reached Earth where they terrorized the human population by burning forests, eating maidens, and squabbling over loot. They were most happy in China. There, the people worshipped them as Rain Gods. It was their squabbling that did them in—along with an embarrassing development. Armored humans, called "knights," rode armored horses and kept sticking them with lances. After a particularly famous knight, Knight George, killed the Amadorian leader Ospumunt, the surviving Amadorians gave up and fled home. A few returned to China every twelve years to honor their dragons."

"During their rather brief stay, Amadorians noticed something about Earth," Dr. Tom explained. "Everything here bred like crazy. High birth rates! If the Amadorians could settle on Earth, they reasoned that they might increase their numbers. Galactic domination might then become possible. So they watched Earth and waited, but they weren't happy with what they saw."

"Humans have a genius for war. A succession of human inventions that included gunpowder, steamships, aircraft, and atomic bombs depressed the Amadorians to the point that they almost gave up! Almost, that is, until humans started carrying animals into orbit. Amadorians saw their chance; if they could change and mutate these animals to make them superior, they reasoned they might be able to recruit them as mercenaries in a war against the humans for possession of Earth."

Hsing-Hsing nodded.

"A few Amadorians might command millions of animals and wipe the humans out. They just wouldn't tell their brave animal soldiers that they planned to eat them later," explained Dr. Tom. "So they positioned satellites with mutagenic rays in the Asteroid Belt and waited. The rays could not penetrate Earth's atmosphere. So only animals in space or very high altitudes were affected first."

"When the animals were changed, the Amadorians got another disappointment," said Dr. Tom. "Very few of the intelligent animals were eager to make war on the humans, since war is not usually an intelligent business."

"There are a few Amadorians you should all know about," said Dr. Tom. "It is the briefing that Laika is passing out to all of you now. With an army like this, only draconian (cruel and severe) discipline assures that they get anything done. Their 'meanness' is their Achilles' heel!"

Kornblend

Fishwick

CHAPTER FIFTEEN

A LITTLE KNOWLEDGE

After the briefing on Amador, it all fell into place. The Zoonauts were fascinated by what they had learned from Hsing-Hsing about these Aliens, but the Zoonauts didn't know what more they could do as a result.

The Aliens were out there in a place where they could not be seen. They came to Earth when they wished. Apparently, the Zoonauts couldn't see their ships, either—at least not on radar. When the Zoonauts got close enough to see them with the naked eye, they were just asking to be shot. Then Mungo came up with an interesting idea.

"If we *could* see their ships, what kind of people would see them?" Mungo asked.

"Well," Methuselah said scratching his feathers with a claw. "All sorts of people."

"And what do they call people who see flying saucers?" asked Mungo.

"Well, they usually call them crazy," replied Methuselah. "But what about the US Air Force? They must see them all the time. But that falls under national security—they wouldn't tell anyone."

"Right," said Mungo. "The US Air Force could be at war with the Amadorians and not tell us. So how do we tell the US Air Force what we now know?"

"We don't," Methuselah said.

Methuselah explained to Mungo the visit from the National Security Agency (NSA) agents, Mr. Christmas and Mr. Valentine. Mungo was so angry that he hopped from one foot to the other and chirped words he didn't usually use around Cody and Jen.

"But that's insane," said Mungo. "Do you mean to say that there's an agency of the government whose job it is to keep people from talking to each other?"

"More than one, I'd guess," said Methuselah. "They're very worried that people will leak secrets to one another."

Methuselah explained to Mungo about spies, counterspies, codes, and decoders. For once, Mungo sat quietly and listened with his full attention. Methuselah told him about the National Security Agency (NSA), the Central Intelligence Agency (CIA), and the Defense Intelligence Agency (DIA), along with the Federal Bureau of Investigation (FBI) and the US Secret Service (USSS).

"But with so many different spy agencies, how do they get anything done?" asked Mungo.

Methuselah laughed.

"A lot of people ask that same question," said Methuselah. "The President created another agency called the Homeland Security Agency (HSA). I am going to talk to Dr. Tom—maybe he and Dr. Brooks know what to do."

Mungo just stared at Methuselah.

"What?" Methuselah asked. "What are you thinking?"

"Ohhhh ...nothing," said Mungo. "But I'll let you know if I come up with any ideas."

With that, Mungo flew off. Methuselah thought he should have followed him as Mungo was prone to finding trouble, but Methuselah was already deep in thought about Jen's friend Sarafina Flores-Abaroa.

Methuselah had met Sara a couple of times when Jen was visiting at her home. It was really Sara's grandmother's home since she was nearly orphaned after her father died and her mother left for Utah. It occurred to Methuselah that special children, like Sara—not the government— were important for the battle with Amador.

Mungo started to disappear for days at a time. Methuselah covered for him for as long as he could, but then he started missing his mandatory exercise flights, too. Methuselah decided it was time to investigate. Of course, he found Mungo in his Command Center in Texas Bob's plastic head.

Mungo and Horace the Owl were sitting before one of the monitors. Both were looking at what appeared to be alphabet soup—random numbers and letters scrolling across the screen. Then Miss Baker the Squirrel Monkey popped out from behind one of Mungo's computers with a wire in one hand and a soldering gun in the other.

"Hello, Methuselah!" Miss Baker said brightly. "Come to help us with the project?"

Mungo and Horace turned suddenly and stared at Methuselah. Both of them appeared horribly guilty.

"Ix-nay on the project-pray," Mungo whispered.

"What project? Methuselah said warily. "What have you been up to?"

"Well...," said Mungo.

"Well...," Horace echoed.

"I think we had best go talk to Dr. Tom," Methuselah said as he had had enough! He had a sinking feeling that he knew what they were doing and just how much trouble they were all in.

Dr. Tom took it better than Methusaleh. He stayed calm, but Methuselah wanted to pluck out all of Mungo's feathers and drop him from a great height. Dr. Tom merely sat and listened until the three culprits were finished talking.

"Let me get this straight," Dr. Tom said. "You've been trying to break the US Air Force's codes so you can get a look at whatever they know about Aliens?"

"Oh no!" Mungo said. "We broke into their codes last week. We're trying to break into. . ."

"Screeeeeeeeeeeeeeeech," howled Horace in a shrill tone while he fixed his stern eyes on Mungo.

"Are you sure you want to get into this?" Horace asked.

"Get into what?" Dr. Tom and Methuselah asked at the same time. Methuselah could only shake his head in disbelief.

Dr. Tom kept his cool. He knew just how to get results.

"Mungo, if you don't tell me everything, I'm going to cut all the wires that lead into your quarters," said Dr. Tom.

"I'm sorry. Okay, Dr. Tom," said Mungo with a shriek and then he hung his head. "I'll tell you everything."

Mungo explained that breaking the US Air Force codes wasn't enough of a challenge. After finding out what the US Air Force knew about Amador, Mungo decided to find out who else knew, so they broke into the NSA Databank in Greenbriar, Virginia.

"That must be the most secure computer in the world," Dr. Tom said. "I'm surprised we don't have NSA agents swarming all over Animalville now. You know they can trace back a break-in."

"We were very careful," Horace confirmed.

"I hope so," said Dr. Tom. "But shut down the hacking operation, now."

Mungo, Horace, and Miss Baker promised they would. Methuselah hoped they were not too late.

When the Zoonauts saw the US Air Force data on Amador, Methuselah almost decided Mungo's little adventure, though not approved, was worth it. The US Air Force had been tangling with Amadorian spacecraft for years. There were dozens of pictures of what the US Air Force decided were scout ships. Oddly, they all looked homemade as if someone had built them in a garage from junkyard parts. They were mostly football- shaped. Each was about fifty feet long, but no two looked alike. They had guns, rocket tubes, and windows oddly placed. Some had designs painted on them. Methuselah was familiar with the Air Force after having served with General Mike. Each plane, helicopter, and missile looked the same, because they were built in factories on assembly lines with identical parts. These Amadorian ships made no sense. Methuselah questioned Hsing-Hsing, whose English was much improved, while Ling-Ling prepared a snack of tasty bamboo shoots.

"Well," Hsing-Hsing started. "First, you must remember that there aren't many of them—only a few thousand. This means they can't do things the way we do on Earth. There are factories on Earth where more than five thousand humans work. That is more than all of the Amadorians. I think each Amadorian has to build his own ship."

"That would explain these pictures," said Methuselah.

"Yes," said Hsing-Hsing. "Their ships are customized like hot rods; like hot rods, they start out as identical cars. I think that these ships did too!"

"Started as cars?" asked Methuselah, puzzled. "I don't get it."

Hsing-Hsing laughed his merry panda laugh. Ling Ling smiled. They were both in love.

"No, but that is the right idea," said Hsing-Hsing. "Notice these ships are all about the same size and shape. They probably had a lot of old ships sitting around, perhaps thousands. Perhaps ships were left over from a war--what humans call 'surplus.' This also suggests there were once more Amadorians."

Methuselah nodded.

"So, we have a few thousand Amadorians in a few thousand very old spaceships who are trying to conquer a planet with five billion people and trillions of animals. They've been trying for how long?" asked Methuselah.

"At least since World War II, possibly longer," said Hsing-Hsing, "if you count the forty or so who came to Earth a thousand years ago who ruled China for a while."

"This doesn't sound like a serious threat," Methuselah said.

Hsing-Hsing munched on a bamboo shoot for a long time before answering.

"But they did take over China for a while," said Hsing-Hsing. "Now they have a few thousand working spaceships with guns and rockets that they can get here. The last time I checked, we had a couple of shuttles and one space station. They are picking off those one at a time. Targeting us is easy for them since we have no guns up there and no rockets, phasers, masers, lasers, photon torpedoes, or defensive shields. Get my point?"

Methuselah fixed his best General Mike flint-and-steel stare on Hsing Hsing.

"We have us," Methuselah said. "I think it's time we did something about it. We have got to get people to listen. The children are the key, and Sara will let us know how. I just know that. It's time to talk with Jen about all of this."

SPACE MILESTONE TIME LINE – 2006 TO 2013

- In **2006,** NASA launched the spaceship New Horizons on the first mission to Pluto, Pluto's moon Charon, and the Kuiper Belt.
- In **2007,** NASA successfully launched four new space science missions designed to improve our understanding of solar processes, the Earth, and the history of the solar system.
- In **2008,** NASA successfully launched six new space and Earth science missions designed to improve our understanding of solar processes, Earth, the universe, and the history of the solar system.
- In **2009,** NASA launched the Wide-Field Infrared Survey Explorer (WISE) spacecraft. By the end of its six-month mission, WISE acquired nearly 1,500,000 images covering the entire sky that will be studied for years to come to answer fundamental questions about the origins of planets, stars, and galaxies and reveal new information about the composition of near Earth objects and asteroids.
- In **2010,** NASA's Hubble Space Telescope's new infrared camera, the Wide Field Camera 3 (WFC3), broke the distance limit for galaxies and uncovered a primordial population of compact and ultra blue galaxies that have never been seen before. Hubble is a powerful "time machine" that allows astronomers to see the most distant galaxies as they were thirteen billion years ago.

- In **2011**, NASA began developing a heavy-life rocket for the human exploration of deep space and helped foster a new era of commercial spaceflight and breakthroughs in technology. Utilizing a newly completed Space Station, major discoveries were made about the universe that will benefit our lives here on Earth.

- In **2013**, NASA helped US commercial companies transform access to low-Earth orbit and the International Space Station; one of the agency's spacecrafts was confirmed to have reached Interstellar Space. Engineers moved ahead to develop technologies that will carry out the first astronaut mission to an asteroid and eventually to Mars.

- In 2014, Gioia Massa who leads the Veggie science team-has been working on the veggie project for years. This team has been experimenting with plants and gardening aboard the Russian space station Mir and NASA's space shuttle. They are very close to resolving gardening problems in a weightless environment.

- In 2015, on September 28th NASA reported there was water on Mars and announced their findings suggest "it would be possible for there to be life today on Mars," according to NASA Mission Chief John Grunsfield. On Mars, each day is 40 minutes longer-and each year has 687 days, compared to 365 on earth.

CHAPTER SIXTEEN
COMPLICATIONS

The Zoonauts were hoping to hear nothing more about Mungo's break-in into the NSA database at Greenbriar, West Virginia, but Mungo was not to be so lucky.

Less than a week later, Mungo and Horace detected and foiled no fewer than nineteen attempts to hack into the Animalville computer systems. After this, the hackers stopped for a while. Mungo was disturbed about the security and his ability to make the Zoonauts' system hacker-proof until Kongo pointed out that had he not hacked into the Greenbriar database he wouldn't be having these problems. Mungo was risking the Zoonauts' financial deals, which especially angered Kongo.

Next, Mungo picked up retargeting instructions to a spy satellite. The Zoonauts all stayed undercover for 10 days as Animalville was photographed from orbit—this meant spies knew their location. Most of the Zoonauts were angry about that.

Then there were problems with aircraft and helicopters nosing around Animalville. Dr. Tom called Dr. Brooks who called an officer at the Johnson Space Center. That officer put through a call to a special US Air Force unit at William Hobby Field. Suddenly, the sky was full of jets;

there were no more troubles with people trying to fly over Animalville—until the Space Shuttle Columbia exploded.

Cars began stopping on Interstate and people began taking pictures of Animalville with telephoto lenses. Laika sent Horace and Plato, the owls, out to get their license numbers. Mungo ran the license numbers through the computer. Most of them turned out to be registered to various government agencies—CIA, DIA, FBI— or not registered at all! So, all vehicles were kept away from Animalville near the Interstate. Dr. Brooks made some calls in Washington. Even those cars stopped visiting.

Then some local residents tried to find out about the Zoonauts. Their exploits were somewhat humorous.

Two FBI agents named Musgrave and Shelton managed to replace the two men who drive the truck that picks up garbage each week. They got as far as the underground parking garage where they found a squad of US Air Force security troops waiting for them. They were returned to the FBI with a warning.

Then a woman named Susan LeBlanc started following Cody home from school. She turned out to be a reporter for *The National Revealer*. When the Air Force driver realized that they were being followed, he radioed the Harris County Sheriff. The Sheriff pulled the woman over and gave her car a ticket for an expired safety inspection. After three days of this, and a $790 fix-it ticket, she finally gave up.

A note about the US Air Force: on one hand, they were carrying on a private "almost war" with Amadorians and not telling the Zoonauts; on the other hand, the US Air Force was responsible for the Zoonauts' safety and security. They usually did a good job. If that sounds confusing, it's because the Air Force and the US Government are very large; just because you are a member of an organization doesn't mean they tell you anything. Dr. Brooks once said that only fourteen people outside of Animalville knew about the Zoonauts, including the president and vice president. The Zoonauts tried to keep it that way. Then an old problem reappeared.

One February night, early in 2003, Nikki the Retriever was out for a walk. It was just after the Space Shuttle Columbia disaster; things at Animalville had just calmed down. Nikki's ability is her acute hearing even at great distances. She usually slept during the day to avoid all the noise. She spent her nights on patrol in Animalville.

Shortly after Jen's school report and Sara's discovery of Animalville, events got even stranger. Early one morning while walking past the Saloon, Nikki heard a break-in taking place. She stopped and listened again. Then she went to find Dr. Tom. She couldn't locate him, so instead she woke up Cody.

"What is it, Nikki?" asked Cody. "It's too early for games."

"Someone is breaking into Animalville," said Nikki. "I can hear it."

"Are you sure?" asked Cody. "There are three fences out there, and all of them are electrified with cameras, too!"

While this was true, the Zoonauts had made a mistake. The cameras were not watched by people, or animals, but by a computer. Computers can be fooled as Mungo often preached.

"Why didn't you tell my Dad?" Cody asked, as he realized this situation was something serious.

"I wanted to, but I couldn't find him anywhere," said Nikki.

"That's because he's away on a special investigation," said Jen.

Cody and Nikki pivoted to see Jen standing in the doorway ready for action.

"This is probably your fault for telling Sara everything the other day," accused Cody.

"That was Methuselah's fault, not mine!" said Jen.

"Well, anyway, it's up to us now to check this out," Nikki advised. Cody pulled on his sweat pants and laced up his sneakers.

Nikki had been reading too much Sherlock Holmes with Author Sir Arthur Conan Doyle—the mystery writer, according to Cody's thinking.

The three of them went out to see what they could find out. They checked one of the cameras by the fence.

"It's sending a fake signal to the camera, so the computer doesn't set off the alarm," Jen said. "This looks like something one of the spy agencies would do."

"I don't think so," said Nikki sniffing around. "There are two sets of footprints—look here. Neither of them is human."

"What are they?" asked Jen.

"Unless I'm wrong, they are a raccoon and a large monkey."

"Oh brother!" said Jen as she rolled her eyes.

"What?" Cody asked in confusion.

"Not you, silly! Don't you see, it must be Bandit and Chuma," announced Jen.

"Precisely," said Nikki.

As Jen picked up the radio, it shattered in her hand. Fragments flew into the darkness. There was a terrible yelp. Nikki was down. Cody ran to Nikki and found her bleeding with a hole in her side. She'd been shot and was going into shock. Cody placed a hand over the wound to stop the bleeding.

"It's all right, old girl," he said. "I'll get you help."

"I don't think so," announced a voice.

Jen and Cody looked up to see Chuma the Chimpanzee step into their flashlight's beam. She was holding a strange-looking weapon pointed right at them.

"Move away from that dog," said Chuma.

"I will not," said Cody pulling off his shirt. He tied it around Nikki, using it as a pressure bandage against the bleeding.

Nikki groaned.

"Sorry, Cody," groaned Nikki.

"It's all right. Don't move. You'll be fine," said Cody.

"It will be all right," said Nikki. "I can hear. I can hear them."

"What?" asked Cody.

"I said move away from the dog," Chuma growled. "I won't say it again."

The weapon was now pointing at Jen's head. With a last look at Nikki, Cody stood up and moved back.

"What do you want here?" Cody said angrily.

Chuma laughed.

"We've come to close this prison," Chuma said.

"But we never mistreated you," said Cody.

"The Amadorians treat us better," Chuma answered. "After they take over, we'll be in charge."

"You'll be food," Jen groaned.

With a snarl, Chuma turned the weapon toward her. Her finger tightened on the trigger.

"That's the last thing you'll ever say, silly girl," warned Chuma.

Then a wonderful thing happened. A huge hand came out of the darkness and snatched the weapon from Chuma's grip. Chuma was suddenly lifted up and face-to-face with Kongo. The Silverback Gorilla shook Chuma violently.

"Give me one reason why I shouldn't crush you like a melon?" asked Kongo.

"Because we don't do that, mate," said Cough Drop the Koala, who stepped out of the darkness and raised his hand.

The scene suddenly brightened. It was as if the sun had risen overhead.

"I found out what I can do," Cough Drop said. "Light and darkness! They are my powers."

"Kongo, don't hurt them," said Jen.

"Why not?" asked Kongo. "We found the other one, the raccoon. He was carrying a bomb; they planned to kill us all."

"Nooooo," gasped Chuma. "Not kill. It's a 'mutagenic' bomb. It's to take away your powers."

There came an angry murmur from every animal. Half of the Animalville population had arrived to help the children, but they weren't in a mood to be nice towards Chuma and Bandit. Cough Drop, as the diplomat, again called for silence.

"Let's think this out, shall we?" asked Cough Drop. "If we kill these two, don't you think those Aliens will just send something worse? Think what we might learn about those space lizards from these hench-beings.

But the most important reason is that this isn't who we are. We're the good guys. We gotta fight the way good guys fight—with honor. Now, I never knew your General Mike, but from all I've heard, I don't think he'd approve, do you?"

Cough Drop had made his point.

There was a murmur of agreement from the animals, and that's when Dr. Angie Stroud drove up with Mungo, Ham the Chimpanzee, and Methuselah atop a motorized gurney.

Ham and Suzy gently lifted Nikki onto the gurney. Dr. Angie checked the bandage Cody had made. Mungo and Ham sped off to the infirmary. Dr. Angie and Methuselah remained behind.

"What'll we do with these two?" Kongo asked.

"Well," said Dr. Angie, "they should have some punishment for being out of bed so late."

"No, not Jen and Cody," said Kongo. "What about the spies?"

"I suppose we should lock them in a storeroom until Dr. Tom and Dr. Brooks can question them," replied Dr. Angie. "We can turn over his gun and that bomb.... Say, where is that bomb?"

"I disarmed it," said Miss Baker the Squirrel Monkey. She proudly waved her favorite tool, a screwdriver.

"You disarmed a mutagenic bomb?" said Cody incredulously.

"We must talk about procedures," added Dr. Angie. "That was a very dangerous thing to do."

Miss Baker shrugged.

"It was a pretty simple bomb, Dr. Angie," said Miss Baker. "It looks like they built it from a bunch of old alarm clocks."

Jen looked at Laika and then at Methuselah.

"Methuselah, what do you think?" asked Jen.

Methuselah shrugged.

"It would make sense if they built it the way they build their ships. I just don't understand how any of their junk is able to work," said Methuselah. "Would it have actually gone off, Miss Baker?"

"I think so," Miss Baker said. "At about dawn."

"When these two would have been far away," said Cody.

"I think we'd better lock them up. Now!" Kongo concluded.

This turned out to be a tragic mistake. The Zoonauts did not realize this at the time – not even Chuma or Bandit. The two rogue animals were locked in a storeroom. While a guard was posted so they couldn't escape, Dr. Angie removed the crystal pellet from Nikki. She announced that the wound was clean and that she would make a full recovery. Some animals went back to bed while others gathered in the Saloon to examine the first Amadorian equipment they had ever seen.

The gun looked like some cross between a high-tech laser and a medieval blunderbuss with rubber rings and gaskets all over it. Miss Baker pointed out all the reasons it shouldn't work as each component was examined.

"It's a mass of solder, screws, and things just plugged into other things. There's even a weld here. These wires look like they wouldn't carry enough electricity to power a toy train, yet they run from the firing mechanism to what must be the battery—this round thing," said Miss Baker. "And this glass tube is not connected to anything, but there's a faint purple light glowing in it. Does this even work?"

"Ask Nikki," Methuselah muttered.

"Oh yeah, it works!" said Nikki. "But I can't tell what it shoots. Light? Heat?"

Cody overturned a small metal tray, and a crystal chip rolled out on top of the table.

"Mom took this out of Nikki," Cody said. "The odd thing is that it is twice as big as the hole it made in Nikki."

"Hmmm," said Kongo.

Kongo picked up a strong magnifying glass and examined the chip closely.

"It's a clear symmetrical crystal," Kongo said. "It is faceted like a cut diamond. It seems to be perfect. I…"

"What is it, Kongo?" asked Methuselah.

"See for yourself," said Kongo.

"It's grown!" said Kongo.

Methuselah and Kongo looked through the magnifier. The chip was twice as large. Cody carefully tipped it back into the metal pan.

"If that kept growing inside Nikki, it would have killed her in a matter of hours," said Jen.

"Well, Dr. Brooks will be here in the morning to collect this, the bomb, and our prisoners," said Kongo. "We'll let the US Government figure out this one."

The Zoonauts all went to bed, but no one slept well that night.

CHAPTER SEVENTEEN
FIRST CONTACT

In the morning, the Zoonauts got a bad shock. While Nikki recovered and was fine, Chuma and Bandit were both dead. There didn't seem to be any cause or reason; they were both just cold. The Zoonauts waited until Dr. Brooks arrived. Then he and Angie performed an autopsy on their bodies. The results were very disturbing.

"We found two little devices, one inside each of them," said Dr. Brooks. "Inside both Chuma and Bandit, as near as we can tell, the Amadorians placed devices there to control their animal 'friends.' When they hadn't returned by dawn, the devices killed them."

"That's terrible," Methuselah said. "But Chuma and Bandit couldn't have known. They never even complained when we locked them up."

"They didn't know," said Jen. "They must have been sacrificed so we couldn't find out anything else."

"See that all the animals are informed," announced Kongo. "I want everyone to realize what kind of creatures we're fighting."

The Zoonauts were talking in the Old Saloon. Besides Dr. Brooks, Dr. Tom, and Methuselah, Jen and Cody were there with Laika, Horace, and Suzy.

"What do you think the Amadorians will do next?" asked Suzy. "Do you think they'll attack Animalville?"

"They might," said Dr. Brooks. "But remember, there aren't very many of them. They may not want to risk getting killed or having us get our hands on one of their ships. They might try to capture more animals instead. At any rate, NASA has decided to station a US Air Force officer here as head of security. They'll select him and he'll arrive in a few weeks."

"And what do we do in the meantime?" asked Methuselah. "They can get around our radar. The US Air Force can't seem to shoot them down. They could show up here at any moment."

"We may have an answer to that," Hsing-Hsing said as he pushed through the doors of the Saloon. "We have discovered what Ling-Ling's power is, but I think we need to go to Kongo's studio to show you."

Ling-Ling followed her mate, true to her shy nature, and the Zoonauts followed Kongo to his studio.

Kongo was waiting in what he called his "studio." It was a large, barnlike building that originally housed maintenance equipment for the park; now it was full of blackboards, computers, virtual reality displays, and file cabinets. Kongo was waiting for the Zoonauts when they arrived and greeted them solemnly. He took science very seriously. It wasn't that he didn't have a sense of humor about other things, but science was his passion.

On the way, Jen grabbed Methuselah by the tail.

"Just why did you tell Sara so much the other day?" Jen asked. "I still can't figure that out. The next day after school, she told me a weird dream that she had about the Zoonauts."

"Shhhh," Methuselah scolded. "As I told you already, Jen, there are things even you don't understand yet. Tell me about the dream later. It could be important if I am right about Sara."

When all the Zoonauts were seated, Kongo tapped a few keys on his computer. The center of the room filled with a three-dimensional model of what Kongo referred to as "*Near Space.*"

"Eight light years in every direction," Kongo said.

"Our sun is at the center."

The star in the center blazed particularly bright.

"Oooooo.....ahhhhh," cooed the Zoonauts all together to express their awe and appreciation.

"I bet even NASA has nothing like this," Cody exclaimed.

"They don't, not yet," said Kongo. "I'll be supplying them with the plans later this month. Hopefully, these will be so inexpensive to produce that we'll be able to put one in every American school."

"Cool!" Cody replied.

"Now then, here is Amador," Kongo continued. He pointed at the screen.

Another light blazed brightly, halfway from the sun to the edge of the display. Then a flashing green line connected the two lights on the screen.

"At light speed, 186,000 miles per second—a speed we cannot even approach—it would take an Amadorian ship about four and a half years to reach Earth. We have reason to believe that they can move far faster than the speed of light."

"Kongo," Dr. Brooks said. The room suddenly became a beehive and buzzed with conversation.

"Yes, Dr. Brooks," Kongo replied.

"You said that you have reason to believe that the Amadorians possess a faster-than-light drive. Can you prove this?"

Kongo chuckled as he had caught Dr. Brooks in a word trap.

"Actually, I said Amadorians can move faster than the speed of light," replied Kongo. "I never said anything about a drive or engine."

"Well, if it is not an engine…," began Dr. Brooks.

Dr. Brooks suddenly turned and stared at the display.

"You saw them," declared Dr. Brooks. "Engine, or not, you saw an Amadorian ship move faster than the speed of light."

"The next best thing," said Kongo. "Ling-Ling."

Ling-Ling rose and waddled to the center of the room. She is a sweet creature, but as ungainly as a grounded duck. She faced the group and then spoke above her usual shyness. Her English had improved greatly.

"As you know, my mate Hsing-Hsing can read Amadorian minds and memories. When they handled us, he absorbed everything that the two Amadorian pilots—Fishwick and Kornblend—thought, knew, or remembered about Amador—experiences, fears, even gossip and legends," said Ling-Ling.

"We have spent most of our time since we came here recording those memories, so we'll know how to fight them. My power is much simpler. I can detect the mental emissions of Amadorians. I know where they are and if they are coming toward us or leaving."

"And what is most remarkable is that time and space seem to be no barrier to her ability," Hsing Hsing added. "We used to think that thought traveled at the speed of light, but we had no clear way to measure it. Now we know that, at least in Ling-Ling's case, thought is instantaneous. She can detect Amadorians, on Amador, over four light years away—now."

There was more buzzing as the animals reacted to that incredible statement. Kongo ignored them and handed Ling-Ling a headset. Ling-Ling placed it over her fuzzy white ears and closed her eyes. Then an amazing thing happened. On the virtual model, there were suddenly lights on the computer screen near the center—Earth. Then, after a few seconds, lights blazed up on the screen all around Amador.

"These lights indicate Amadorians," said Kongo. "Notice a few lights off here and there. We believe that those are scout ships. Watch when I increase the magnification of the Earth and our Solar System."

Suddenly the Earth was the size of a large marble with a brilliant, basketball-sized sun in the background.

"Sorry," muttered Kongo.

Kongo turned down the brilliance on the computer screen so that the sun's light would not blind the Zoonauts. When the Zoonauts vision returned, they could see three bright lights around Earth, one on the Moon, and a cluster of eight or nine some distance away.

"What are those? Amadorians?" asked Cody.

"Yes, mostly in pairs," replied Kongo, indicating the cluster of bright lights. "In scout ships we think. We're not exactly sure what this is."

"Where is that?" asked Cody.

"The asteroid belt, near the star Ceres," said Kongo. "Why? Do you think you know what it is?"

Cody walked around the model and studied it.

"Stop showing off," said his sister Jen.

Cody made a face at her.

"I'm not," retorted Cody. "That's a forward base, like a Death Star. That way the Amadorian scouts don't have to go all the way back to Amador for hot food and fuel—or baths, if they wash!"

"If that's true," Methuselah said. "Then Amadorians are very serious about their mission on Earth. In World War II, we built forward bases all the way across the Pacific. It's what you do when you want to conquer a country, colony, or planet."

"The only question is, what do we do about it?" asked Cody.

As it turned out, almost the very first thing the Zoonauts did about their new discovery was the paperwork. Dr. Brooks handed each Zoonaut a stack of secrecy agreements that each animal "signed" with a mark. Dr. Brooks and Dr. Tom witnessed the papers. Each Zoonaut agreed if they told anyone about anything concerned with Animalville—Aliens or the US Government—then they could be placed in prison for the rest of their lives. Some of the animals were offended until Kongo reminded them that the Zoonauts were at war and had chosen sides. The humans weren't asking anything of the Zoonauts that they weren't asking of each other.

Methuselah thought about Sara and all that he had told her; he flew over to Dr. Tom and landed on his shoulder for a private conference.

"Dr. Tom," Methuselah whispered. "There is something else that you should know about. A few days ago, Jen told her friend Sara that I could talk. It was sort of an accident, so please don't be angry with her. We met for an emergency Zoonaut counsel; I was nominated to tell Sara our history."

"But why, Methuselah?" asked Dr. Tom.

"As we discussed the crisis, Ling-Ling got an image of Sara in her mind," said Methuselah. "Sara was sleeping on top of a large key. None of us could figure out that vision, but we all decided Sara must be important and should join us. Just before this meeting, Jen told me that Sara had a dream about us, but I don't know yet what it is about."

Dr. Tom turned to his daughter Jen.

"Jen, I think we have to talk," said Dr. Tom. "Follow me!"

The two departed the conference room.

"It is probably time for you to invite your friend Sara over for a visit," said Dr. Tom.

Jen was terrified. She wondered if Methuselah had betrayed her?

The Alien gun, bomb, and the bodies of Chuma and Bandit were shipped off to a US Government lab. The Zoonauts never saw them again. In the meantime, the Zoonauts waited for the Amadorians to show up again. Ling-Ling spent much of her time at Kongo's lab tracking the Amadorians. Usually, there was one in orbit somewhere above Animalville. The US Air Force could never track it. The cloaking device the Amadorians used to shield their ships from radar was effective.

Then a series of events occurred that brought about a face-to-face meeting with the Aliens!

In March, the Zoonauts decided to send a delegation to Cape Canaveral, Florida. Jen and Cody were given a full battery of medical tests and scans to see if growing up with the Animalville gang had changed them as well. The tests, though they were not told, were the first tests used to screen potential Zoonauts as astronauts.

Kongo's daughter Patty Cake would be going for special tests. Her ability to move herself (psychokinesis) and objects (telekinesis) using only her mental powers was very strong. Dr. Brooks wanted to find out just how powerful she was. Patty Cake was to meet a few NASA officials who needed convincing.

Sara had revisited Animalville and repeated her dream to Dr. Tom. Sara had recently had a second unusual dream, but was not sure what it was all about. It was really a nightmare—in it there was a large, bulbous pod plant that resembled a Venus flytrap. These plants were arranged in a single row straining upward to get a ray of light through a dim, unearthly sky.

Sara instinctively knew that the plants were dangerous killers although she had no idea where they came from. Their flowers had razor-sharp teeth, and she woke up in a cold sweat just as one of them leaped viciously toward her. Sara even woke up her Grandmother Flores with her screams. Was her imagination getting the best of her? Had she watched too many horror movies? Sara decided to visit Animalville again soon.

All the exposure bothered Dr. Brooks. As far as he was concerned, too many people knew about Animalville already. He expressed his concern often and frequently would say: "Every morning when I open the paper, I expect to see the Zoonauts on the front page. If this gets much more out of hand, they'll be hosting the Macy's Thanksgiving Day Parade."

Finally, the group was scheduled to return to Cape Canaveral, Florida, with the new United States Air Force Chief of Security for Animalville, Major Davis Prescott.

Prescott would pilot the team back in an Air Force jet, but no one had briefed the Major about Animalville as yet. The Zoonauts hoped that when he learned about their unique abilities, he would not take the news too hard.

Meanwhile, the Amadorians had other plans!

CHAPTER EIGHTEEN

FLORIDA

Major Davis Prescott was not a happy man. He stood at attention before the desk of General Roysmith who was the US Air Force officer responsible for dealing with NASA. Roysmith was reviewing Major Prescott's file.

"You have a first-class record, Major," said General Roysmith.

"Thank you, sir," replied Major Prescott.

"How long have you been in B-52s?" asked General Roysmith.

"Eighteen months, sir," answered Major Prescott. "I was hoping to stay with my current assignment."

Prescott thought to himself, "Not long enough." He waited for the general to respond.

"I know you were hoping to stay in your current assignment," General Roysmith continued. "Relax, Major, at ease."

Prescott slumped slightly.

"Why am I being taken out of the Flying Squadron, sir?" asked Major Prescott. "If there's a problem with my performance…"

"There's no problem, Major Prescott," General Roysmith replied. "It's just that we have a new assignment for you. This is a promotion opportunity. Make no bones about it—this is a tough job. But if you do it well, there will be a silver leaf at the end for you—a promotion to lieutenant colonel."

A silver leaf. Major Prescott contemplated the gold leaf on his shoulders. Promotion meant more responsibility if he was awarded the rank of lieutenant colonel.

Prescott groaned. He didn't want a promotion—he just wanted to fly.

"Comment, Major?" asked General Roysmith.

"No, sir. I mean, yes, sir," said Major Prescott. "If it's all the same to the General."

"No, it isn't," replied General Roysmith as his smile disappeared. "This isn't an offer. It's an order. You will take up the post of Security and Liaison Officer at Site Lucky Bravo (the Air Force code name for Animalville) effective immediately. Do I make myself clear?"

"Yessir," replied Major Prescott.

"Listen, Prescott," cautioned General Roysmith. "This may be the most important security assignment since the Manhattan Project. If this works out, you may have a chance at changing history. Don't take it lightly."

General Roysmith tossed a sealed envelope on the desk.

"Your orders, Major," said General Roysmith.

Major Prescott picked up the envelope.

"Sir," Major Prescott stated with a salute.

"Now get out to the flight line," said General Roysmith.

"The flight line, sir?" asked Major Prescott.

"Yes, you're still a pilot, aren't you?" asked General Roysmith. "Dismissed. Good luck!"

"That was horrible," said Cody.

"Don't be a baby," said Jen.

"You're telling me you liked it?" asked Cody.

"No one likes a CAT Scan," replied Jen.

Jen and Cody had just finished their NASA physicals. The final event was a fifteen-minute ride through the noisy, vibrating CAT Scan tunnel. Cody was wondering if he might be claustrophobic, but probably not. He just hated to be still for fifteen minutes.

"You know what that was for?" asked Jen in a whisper as they followed the winding corridors back to the visitor's lounge.

"Yeah. They wanted to see if the animals have changed us," replied Cody. "Maybe they thought we were becoming 'were-monkeys' or something."

Jen looked at her brother with tremendous impatience.

"You're such a doofus," Jen stated. "What is a 'were-monkey,' anyway?"

"Some kind of monster—you know, like a werewolf, duh!" retorted Cody. "So really, what have you heard?"

Jen had enough of Cody and began to look for a way to lose him.

"No, a nurse told me," replied Jen.

"Told you what?" asked Cody.

"She asked if we'd won some kind of contest," explained Jen. "When I told her 'No,' then she said, 'You must be very important because the full NASA astronaut physical is very expensive.'"

Cody stopped dead in his tracks.

"Astronaut physical?" Cody said. "You are kidding, right?"

"That's what she said," Jen affirmed with a nod.

"Do you suppose?" asked Cody.

"Why not?" said Jen.

"That's impossible," said Cody.

Jen stopped and stared at her brother.

"I stopped using the word 'impossible' the first time a talking gorilla helped me with my math and science homework," Jen reprimanded.

Laika and Patty Cake waited in a special Security Loading Area. Patty Cake eyed the large metal cage distastefully.

"I didn't ride in a cage on the way down here," Patty Cake said.

"No," said Laika. "But Dr. Brooks piloted the plane on the way down. The new security officer is flying us back, and he doesn't know about the Zoonauts yet."

"Well, he's certainly going to find out about the Zoonauts team when he arrives, isn't he?" asked Patty Cake.

Laika nodded.

"Yes, and I expect that it'll be quite a shock to him," said Laika. "He may get nervous, tense, and perhaps he may even faint. Now would you rather have him do that before or after he flies us halfway across the United States?"

"After, of course," said Patty Cake with a sulk. "But I still don't like the cage."

"Unfortunately, that's the way things are," Laika reminded her. "Relax. It's only for a few hours, and then we'll be home."

A door opened. Jen and Cody walked in. Laika looked up.

"Hi, kids," said Laika. "Want to play Frisbee?"

"Guess what?" asked Cody. "They gave us astronaut physicals."

"Ah, yes. I knew they were going to do that," said Laika.

"You could have told us," scolded Cody.

Laika sat down and scratched thoughtfully.

"You weren't supposed to know yet," said Laika. "We may or may not need you to go into space. We don't know how dangerous it will be!"

"Cool!" said Cody.

Jen had a different opinion.

"Were they planning to ask us if we wanted to go, or were we going to be drafted?" Jen asked.

"I wanna go," declared Cody.

"Well, I might want to go to college, or do something else," said Jen.

"Or get married?" asked Cody.

Jen had been dating a boy from school, and Cody loved to tease her about it.

"Jen's going to get married to Billy Thurlow and be a housewife," teased Cody in a loud whisper to Laika. "She can't wait."

"I'm sure that if NASA wants any of us to go into space—or go back into space, they will ask us," said Laika with a nod toward Patty Cake, "If it means saving the planet, I, for one, will go."

"Me, too," said Cody.

"And me," declared Patty Cake.

"Well, I will think it over, *if* they ask me," said Jen.

With a whir of motors, the great hangar doors began to roll back. Laika shooed Patty Cake back into her cage and latched it as bright lights flooded the loading area. Outside the hangar stood the new, sleek, executive jet. Men came in to push Patty Cake's cage toward the plane as Jen, Cody, and Laika walked alongside.

There was a US Air Force major standing by the doorway to the plane. Jen and Cody decided he must be the new security officer.

"Jennifer and Cody Stroud?" asked Major Prescott. He held a clipboard with his passenger manifest and checklist.

"That's Jen and I'm Cody. This is Laika," said Cody. "That is Patty Cake."

Laika sat at Jen's heel looking like a normal dog.

Major Prescott turned to see the aircrew push a cage from the lift into the cargo door of the plane. Inside, an unhappy Patty Cake looked back at him.

"I'm going to have a huge monkey on my plane?" Major Prescott said in angry surprise.

"Not a monkey," said Jen. "A gorilla...and she is very ...uhmm... calm."

"She doesn't look calm," said Major Prescott grinding his teeth.

"Neither do you, and you're flying this plane," said Cody under his breath.

Major Prescott looked at Cody with contempt.

"What?" Major Prescott asked.

"Nothing," said Cody. "Can we go on board?"

Major Prescott nodded and then watched as the kids and Laika boarded the plane. He shook his head and thought: "What crazy deal did I get myself into this time?"

Major Prescott and the Zoonauts flew west across the Florida, Panhandle toward Houston. There was a large storm gathering above the Mississippi River Delta between Cape Canaveral, Florida and Animalville. Huge thunderheads and storm clouds were rearing up above the land and moving south into the Gulf of Mexico. The little executive jet was heading straight into the storm.

Major Prescott was at the controls and letting the plane fly on autopilot. He listened to the weather report with half an ear. Cody sat beside him as copilot. Cody was far too young to be a pilot, but he had talked the Major into giving him a flight lesson. Major Prescott watched the developing storm. He was bored and even a little resentful. He glanced at Cody at the controls next to him.

"Easy on the stick, son," said Major Prescott to Cody. "She'll fly herself if you let her. That's the way she's built."

Major Prescott glanced out the window. Biloxi, Mississippi was far below them. Clouds covered much of the Gulf.

"Some job for a decorated combat pilot, huh?" Major Prescott said to Cody.

"You don't like working for NASA?" Cody asked.

Major Prescott glanced at Cody.

"As what? An Air Force taxi driver for a bunch of zoo animals?" Major Prescott said. "Fooey!"

"They're not zoo animals," Cody said stubbornly. "They're all NASA spaceflight veterans!"

Major Prescott scowled as he remained unconvinced of his good fortune.

"Hey, Major, cheer up," said Cody. "Maybe they'll let you fight a war somewhere."

"That's not funny," Major Prescott retorted. "You shouldn't joke about things like that."

"Duh!" said Cody. "Lighten up, sir!"

"Kids!" Major Prescott said with a sigh.

The kids and Zoonauts made Major Prescott wonder if he could get a transfer to the US Navy.

Back in the passenger area, Jen Stroud and Laika were sitting facing each other in opposite seats. They looked out the window when the 'Fasten Seat Belt' sign came on. Lightning flashed outside the window, and Jen cringed.

"I hate flying through storms," said Jen.

"Modern air travel is relatively safe in any weather," Laika said thoughtfully. "Now, if you want a frightening flight, I recommend high-angle orbital reentry. Very nasty."

Jen shuddered at the thought.

"I'll pass for now," Jen said. "Are you okay, Patty Cake?"

Jen looked back at Patty Cake who was in the back of the plane in the cargo area, curled up in her large cage wearing a gloomy expression.

"I hate this cage," whined Patty Cake. "Why can't I sit on the seat? Laika is on the seat."

"Because I am a dog," replied Laika. "Dogs sit on seats. Major Prescott doesn't know about us, and humans are afraid of gorillas. You saw the movie *King Kong*!"

"King Kong was framed!" said Patty Cake.

A bolt of lightning rocked the plane, causing all three of them to cry out in surprise. Then the intercom buzzed and startled Jen a second time. It was Cody on the intercom.

"Cool storm, huh?" asked Cody. "You okay back there?"

"No," Jen cried. "I'm not. I hate storms. Can't we go around it?"

"No way, Sis—but we can go over it," Cody said. "Hang on."

The intercom went dead.

"Hang on?" exclaimed Patty Cake. "What does he mean, 'hang on'?"

At that moment, they felt the plane climb, and Patty Cake gripped the bars of her cage and gritted her teeth.

"I still hate storms," Jen shouted.

But as the jet swiftly rose above the clouds, something larger, rounder, and more menacing was flying above it—something invisible to their radar—an Amadorian spacecraft!

Crammed in the little cockpit amid gauges, lights, dials, levers, wheels, food wrappers, and Earth magazines, the two Amadorians were trying to line up their range finders on the jet. Fishwick fought the controls as the storm bounced the ungainly scout ship around.

"It's them! It's them!" Kornblend yelped.

"Are you sure?" Fishwick asked.

Kornblend thumped a piece of equipment with a lighted screen on the side. The screen flickered, and then the picture came back.

"Be careful," Fishwick ordered. "That equipment is delicate."

"Right," said Kornblend. "Well, it says that the dog creature Laika is in that plane. Get closer! I'll blast them."

"You idiot!" said Fishwick. "We're supposed to bring the dog back alive and well. The *Big Lizard* wants to study it."

Kornblend looked at his partner, and his mind turned over this incomprehensible idea.

"Why?" Kornblend asked.

"So they can learn how to take over Earth," replied Fishwick.

"Oh...why not just blast Earth?" asked Kornblend.

"Because...," Fishwick explained patiently, "Earth will wind up looking like Amador if we do, you bonehead!"

A light seemed to go on in Kornblend's dense mind.

"Oh, good reason," said Kornblend. "I'll just target their engines."

"You do that," said Fishwick.

As the little jet pulled out above the clouds, the Zoonauts hit calmer air and the plane leveled off. Major Prescott decided to call in their position.

"Houston, this is NASA One-Niner," said Major Prescott. "We are less than one-half hour out. Request landing clearance. Over."

Just at that moment, about a half mile above them, Kornblend was peering into his targeting scope. As he pressed the trigger, he spoke in his imitation action-figure accent the words he had adopted as his own battle cry.

"Hasta la vista, baby!" cried Kornblend.

A beam of electrical energy lanced down and struck the jet engines below. Inside the cockpit of the NASA One-Niner, Major Prescott and Cody ducked away as the plane was suddenly bathed in a brilliant light.

"What was that?" asked Cody. "Lightning?"

But Prescott heard the bang as the engines blew out.

"I don't think so," said Major Prescott.

All the dials on the console dropped to zero. Alarms began to sound as Major Prescott reached for the controls and grabbed the yoke of the plane.

"Something hit us!" said Major Prescott. "We've got no engines! Buckle up and hang on!"

Major Prescott wrestled the controls as the plane nosed over and started dropping fast. Cody grabbed for the radio microphone.

"Houston this is NASA One-Niner," Cody announced. "We're going down!"

Cody looked at Major Prescott.

"Where are we going down?" Cody asked.

"The Atchafalaya Swamp," replied Major Prescott. "Somewhere… east of New Iberia."

Cody repeated their location into the radio as they hurtled down through the thundering clouds toward the bayou below.

In the rear compartment, Patty Cake clutched the bars of her cage and Jen tightened her seat belt. Laika slid up against the forward bulkhead.

"I thought you said this was safe!" cried Jen.

"I said, 'relatively safe!'" Laika replied, as he was now upside down against the cabin wall.

Cody and Major Prescott watched as the plane suddenly dropped below the clouds. The plane screamed low over the Louisiana bayou and passed the treetops.

"It's going to be a water landing," said Major Prescott through clenched teeth.

NASA One-Niner belly-landed on the water with rooster tails of spray as it skipped like a stone toward the forest and just missed a tree.

"Yaaaaaaahhhhhh!" yelled Major Prescott.

The plane shot between two trees and clipped off it's wings before it came to rest in a tree-shaded pool where it began to sink.

The Amadorian spacecraft cruised overhead and searched for the plane a few seconds later.

"I don't see it," said Kornblend.

"Keep looking," said Fishwick. "It has to be down there somewhere."

The Amadorian spacecraft disappeared over the trees.

The US Air Force jet, its cargo doors now open, was slowly filling with water.

Nearby, Major Prescott, Jen, Cody, Laika, and Patty Cake huddled out of the rain on a tiny, one-tree island.

Major Prescott looked around.

"We'll be all right now," said Major Prescott. "The plane has a radio transmitter, so it should lead them right to us."

"If that freak bolt of lightning didn't knock it out," said Cody.

"If it was lightning," said Major Prescott looking at Cody. "Kid, if it knocked out the transmitter, then it probably knocked out the cockpit radio, too. That means that no one heard our distress call."

"Rats," said Cody.

Patty Cake suddenly saw something and tapped on Jen's shoulder. They both turned to see an Amadorian ship cruise by a hundred yards away. Jen looked at Patty Cake.

"Is that what I think that is?" asked Jen.

Patty Cake nodded.

They were lost in a swamp in the rain with space monsters tracking them. Patty Cake's only wish now was that she was back in her clean, dry cage.

**Atchafalaya Swamp, Louisiana
(Sara's Dream Comes True)**

CHAPTER NINETEEN

BACK IN ANIMALVILLE

The same storm that was drenching the Louisiana swamp was just starting to move through Texas. The sky was almost black when the first few raindrops began to fall on the streets of Animalville. Most of the animals went inside to get out of the rain; a few, like the frogs and toads, came out to enjoy the shower. Inside the lighted windows of the Stroud Veterinary Clinic, there were happy puppy noises.

Dr. Tom was examining a small Husky-Shepherd puppy named Laika Junior. Junior was reacting with enthusiastic affection to Dr. Tom's attention. He wiggled and woofed. His mother, Heisler, watched proudly from the couch.

"Good boy. Good Junior," said Heisler. "Too bad Jen and Cody aren't here to see you."

"He's just fine," said Dr. Tom turning to Heisler with a smile.

Heisler wagged her tail.

"That is good," Heisler said. "His daddy will be so pleased. I wish he was here, too!"

Heisler wrinkled her brow in concern.

"They all will be back in a few hours and should even arrive before suppertime," assured Dr. Tom. "The new security officer is flying them in from Florida."

Heisler laughed.

"Is he going to be in for a shock!" Heisler exclaimed.

"Perhaps Dr. Brooks briefed him before he left," said Dr. Tom. He set Junior back on the floor who then bustled back to Heisler and climbed up on the couch.

"Even if he did," Heisler said, "It'll still be a shock. Where's Dr. Angie tonight?"

Junior yipped and wiggled as Heisler played with him.

"She is in Washington, DC, attending a conference on endangered animal species," said Dr. Tom.

Heisler laughed and Junior yipped and butted his head with hers.

"If the Aliens have their way, we'll all be endangered," Heisler said.

Across the room, Mungo the Parrot sat before a computer console and played a lightning fast game of cards, pecking like a machine. Luna the Cat paused while grooming herself to give him a disapproving look.

"You spend far too much time in front of that thing," said Luna. "You are going to ruin your eyes."

"Ha!" squawked Mungo. "The future is electronic. This is the e-tech era."

"Perhaps, but you are going to look funny wearing glasses," said Luna.

The phone rang, and Dr. Tom picked it up.

"Clinic, Dr. Tom Stroud. Yes? Where?" asked Dr. Tom.

Everything in the clinic stopped as the animals caught the worried tone in Dr. Tom's voice and turned to listen.

"Can you tell me anything else?" Dr. Tom asked. "Okay, thank you."

Dr. Tom turned to Mungo and dispatched him with orders.

"Mungo, get Kongo, now!" said Dr. Tom.

"Trouble, Chief?" asked Mungo.

"The kids' plane went down," explained Dr. Tom. "Hurry!"

A hundred feet below in the parking garage, Sara Flores-Abaroa was parking her bike. She had to tell someone about her most recent dream. Sara was still shaken by the image of a plant leaping at her. Then, holding her precious security pass which she had received ten days earlier, she walked toward the elevator and thought how much her life had changed forever. After another guard examined the pass, she got into the elevator.

Mungo was out the door like a shot. He flew between raindrops as he streaked across Main Street of Animalville and passed two curious chimps clad in raincoats riding their bicycles.

Mungo entered the Arcade and zoomed past Horace the Owl who squawked in irritation and dropped his newspaper. Mungo flew to the Old Funhouse Ride where the primates now made their home and looked around frantically.

"The plane's gone down," Mungo shouted. "The plane!"

Then Mungo realized he was talking only to himself. He looked around. Gina the Orangutan was welding a freestanding metal sculpture.

She pushed back her welder's helmet and turned off the torch. Mungo zoomed up and hovered in front of her face.

"Where's Kongo?" Mungo demanded.

"Where he always is—in his lab," Gina replied

"Thankya, thankya very much!" said Mungo in his best Elvis Presley imitation and flew off.

"Silly bird," mumbled Gina.

Ham the Chimpanzee stuck his head out of the bathroom at that moment with his mouth full of toothpaste and a toothbrush stuck in his mouth.

"What was that all about?" Ham asked. He tried not to drool toothpaste down his cheek.

"I dunno," replied Gina. "Something about a plane crash..."

"What?" Ham exploded. Water sprayed and toothpaste went everywhere.

Before Gina could reply, Ham was gone.

In the center of Kongo's lab, dozens of lighted particles circled though the air and formed a complex theoretical matrix. It was a holographic representation of Kongo's latest theory. It was also quite pretty.

Kongo, the huge Silverback Gorilla, and Laika the Russian Dog were the leaders of Animalville. He now stood watching this matrix while adjusting it on a small handheld keyboard. Occasionally, he paused to poke his glasses back onto his flat nose.

"Uhmmmmm," Kongo said. "Hmmmmmmm, uh huh."

Kongo turned to chalk down some numbers and symbols on a blackboard. Mungo flew in at that moment and perched on the end of a telescope, which dropped under his weight and collided with the table it stood on.

"Be careful of that!" growled Kongo. "It's delicate."

"The plane, Boss...the plane!" Mungo shrieked.

"What are you babbling about?" asked Kongo still focused on his lighted matrix.

"The plane, the one coming back from Florida with the kids!" Mungo gasped. After he caught his breath he spoke in his normal voice. "It's gone down in a Louisiana swamp."

"*What?*" Kongo bellowed. His fingers crushed the keyboard with an involuntary clench of his fist and all the moving specks of light stopped midair and went out as they dropped to the floor.

A moment later, the outer wall of the old Maintenance Building that housed Kongo's lab began to bulge. Then it exploded outward as Kongo ran through it. He headed to the airstrip with Mungo flying behind him. A few seconds later, Ham the Chimpanzee appeared in the opening where the wall once stood with toothpaste streaking from his mouth.

"Hey, wait for me!" Ham shouted.

On the airstrip, a big heavy-lift helicopter was warming up its rotor blades. Its door opened. The pilot was an Orangutan named Percy. Percy insisted that everyone call him "Race" after a cartoon character he admired since he had learned to fly. Dr. Tom didn't mind as Race was a terrific pilot. Cough Drop, a radio headset squashed down over his bush hat, sat in the copilot's seat. He was learning to fly from Race although his small Koala arms and legs needed blocks to mechanically extend his reach to the controls.

"Here he comes!" squawked Mungo as he flew past Dr. Tom, waiting by the copter door, and announced Kongo's arrival.

As Kongo boarded the copter, Dr. Tom joined the crew to brief them.

"Now don't panic," said Dr. Tom. "Spysat One has their plane pinpointed and we'll get them out."

Kongo was close to having a full gorilla meltdown, but controlled his voice well, considering his daughter was aboard the downed plane.

"Considering that my only daughter is lost in a swamp, I think I'm being remarkably calm," confessed Kongo.

"Hey, wait for me," said Ham, running up the tarmac to the plane as Tom and Kongo turned toward him.

"Just what we need," groaned Kongo who was not happy to see the gangly teenage chimpanzee. "What are you doing here?"

"If Patty Cake's in trouble, I'm going!" Ham said.

"No, you're not!" Kongo bellowed.

Dr. Tom got the last word.

"Kongo, we need Ham," Dr. Tom explained. "His abilities may come in handy."

Kongo looked angrily at Ham who stood his ground and stuck out his jaw.

"Kids!" said Kongo. "How do we survive them? Very well, but if he does anything…"

"I won't!" cried Ham as he boarded the copter.

"Wait!" cried Sara.

Tom turned to see Sara riding up on one of the base bicycles. She was followed by Gina the Orangutan, two chimps, and Horace the Owl.

"I want to help," cried Sara. "There is something I have to tell you. I had another dream and it really scared me!"

"We have no time to talk now," said Dr. Tom. "This mission is off-limits to civilians."

Dr. Tom looked at Sara who seemed desperate to participate in something important.

"Go back to the clinic and take care of Heisler," Dr. Tom instructed. He winked at Gina the Orangutan. "Heisler just had pups, and you are in charge until we get back."

The copter rocketed straight up into the dark sky.

Sara stood, watched their departure. She was bitterly disappointed until Gina put her long arm around her shoulder.

"Oh Gina, won't anyone listen to me?" asked Sara.

"Yes, honey, I'm here," said Gina. "Now, what is this dream all about? Did you eat something before bedtime? That always gives me bad dreams."

"No, I think it is something that is going to happen, or maybe it already happened, or...," Sara blurted out in a jumbled state of confusion. "I don't know!"

"Well, come on," said Gina the Orangutan. "Tell me all about it, and maybe we can figure something out. Let's see what we can do to help with this new Heisler puppy, Junior, in the meantime!"

Sara and Gina cycled back to the Veterinary Clinic to wait for word from Dr. Tom and the Zoonauts' flight rescue crew.

CHAPTER TWENTY

MEANWHILE, DOWN IN THE BOONDOCKS

With a burping noise, the tail of NASA One-Niner aircraft disappeared under the surface of the dirty, murky swamp. The little plane was gone.

"Hope they don't take that out of your pay," Cody muttered to Major Prescott.

"I didn't blow the engines out of that plane," Major Prescott replied gloomily. "Something hit us."

"Not lightning?" asked Cody.

"No way," replied Major Prescott.

As the rain pelted down, the five survivors huddled under their single tree and tried to stay dry. Major Prescott stayed as far away from Patty Cake as he could. Jen turned to Cody and told him it was time for action.

"We've got to do something," Jen whispered to Cody. "There are Amadorians out there looking for us."

"What?" asked Cody.

"Patty Cake and I saw one of their scout ships a few minutes ago," said Jen.

"Oh, no!" said Cody as he slumped down against the tree trunk. "Who? What?"

Laika's paw was on Cody's arm and Cody looked into the dog's questioning eyes. Putting his lips near Laika's ear, Cody passed on the bad news.

"Why are you whispering to a dog?" Major Prescott asked.

"Because it's a secret," Cody said flippantly with the hope that Major Prescott would take him for being a wise guy and not push the matter.

"A secret?" questioned Major Prescott.

"Yeah," replied Cody.

"To a dog?" asked Major Prescott.

"That's right," said Cody.

"Dogs can't talk," said Major Prescott.

"Then he probably won't tell anyone," replied Cody.

Major Prescott scowled and bit back his reply. Then he just shook his head.

"Well, someone has to do something," said Major Prescott.

The Major rose to his feet and pulled out his service pistol.

"Whoa, Major," said Jen. "What are you going to do with that?"

"I'm going to fire a few shots," said Major Prescott. "Maybe someone will hear it and come get us."

Jen jumped to her feet.

"I have a better idea," Jen offered. "Patty Cake, can you climb this tree and see if you can tell where we are?"

Patty Cake looked at Jen and nodded. She climbed up the nearest tree and out of sight. Major Prescott watched with doubt as she scrambled up through the tree branches. He tilted his head back and looked up.

"What can she tell us if she does?" asked Major Prescott. "She's a monkey!"

Laika rolled his eyes.

"She's a gorilla!" snapped Jen in an offended tone. "And a very smart one!"

Major Prescott threw up his hands.

"My mistake," he said. "That makes all the difference."

Patty Cake climbed to the top of the tree. Instead of looking around, she closed her eyes and touched a finger to her temple. Instantly, her powers became active. Unlike the other animals, Patty Cake had more than one ability. The Strouds and Kongo were still trying to determine just how gifted a gorilla she would prove herself to be with her powers. There was no telling how many powers she possessed. However, one of her powers was her ability to "Far-See." Patty Cake could see a person or an object that was far away, or out of sight. With the use of her intuition, she knew what to focus on. Patty Cake had seen the Amadorian ship cruise by and she knew what to look for and where to find it.

Patty Cake narrowed her vision of the distance by half while the scene wavered. As she focused in on the scene, the colors washed out to gray. Then, with a blur of speed, suddenly there appeared a dot of brilliant color. With a blink, Patty Cake refocused. She cut the distance in half again from the object of her focus. In her mind, her vision revealed the Amadorian spacecraft sitting on a small island. Patty Cake frowned with her eyes still closed.

"From bad to worse," muttered Patty Cake. "What next?"

In Patty Cake's vision, the Amadorian spacecraft was sitting on that island clumsily camouflaged with moss and branches. The door opened and out stepped Fishwick and Kornblend who were dressed like foot soldiers. They carried battle lasers and wore body armor that made them look like rejects from a road warrior film. Fishwick was furious and turned a withering glance at his partner.

"I can't believe you shot it down," said Fishwick.

"I just targeted the engines like you said," Kornblend replied, sulking.

"Then how come it didn't hover," asked Fishwick.

"Maybe Earth ships don't hover," said Kornblend.

"Don't be ridiculous," replied Fishwick. "They must hover. We've seen Earth ships hover. If they don't hover, how can they loiter? Or lurk?"

Fishwick kicked at a chunk of earth, but merely scatted mud on his leg. Kornblend powered up his laser and tried to look fierce.

"Their ship crashed over there," said Kornblend. "Let's just go get the dog."

"What if the dog isn't alone?" asked Fishwick. "What if there are others?"

Fishwick's mood brightened considerably.

"In that case, we can eat them," Fishwick said. "Remember what the Amadorian Codex says in Chapter VII, Verse 39: 'The friend of your enemy is your enemy as well; if he is your enemy, you may eat him as well, preferably in a nice light wine sauce.' I wonder how they taste? I'm getting awfully tired of dried frink fruit and iguana jerky."

"We can eat them, then?" asked Kornblend.

"Yes," replied Fishwick.

"Good," said Kornblend.

Kornblend brandished his laser threateningly and recited, in his best action hero imitation, which wasn't very good, his favorite ultimatum.

"Do you feel lucky, punk?" asked Kornblend.

His long-suffering partner Fishwick shook his head.

"You have got to stop watching Earth action features," warned Fishwick. "Come on."

The two, loaded for trouble, waded off the island and headed for the downed plane.

Major Prescott leaned against the tree while it rained, and he became drenched and impatient. Looking at the pool where the plane had gone down, the US Air Force officer missed Patty Cake as she lowered herself out of the tree and dropped to the ground behind him.

"This is getting us nowhere," Major Prescott groused.

Patty Cake chose that moment to tap him on the shoulder, and Major Prescott almost jumped out of his clothes.

"Don't do that!" he yelled.

As Major Prescott backed away from Patty Cake, Jen asked her, "What did you see?!"

Patty Cake glanced uncomfortably at Major Prescott and then shrugged. She then began an elaborate attempt to reply in sign language. Major Prescott bent down to Cody to whisper in his ear while his eyes still guarded Patty Cake's every move.

"What's she saying?" asked Major Prescott.

"I have no idea," Cody said. "Jen, this isn't working."

Jen looked helplessly at Laika, who shrugged and gave up the deception.

"Patty Cake, perhaps you had better deliver your report verbally," Laika said.

Major Prescott's eyes grew as large as quarters since he did not believe what he had just heard.

"A talking dog?" asked Major Prescott. "What is this, a trick?"

Major Prescott turned angrily in disbelief toward Cody.

"This is no time for games, Cody," Major Prescott scolded. "How did you do that?"

"He didn't," said Patty Cake with a sigh. "I'm a ventriloquist."

"The monkey, too?" cried Major Prescott.

"Gorilla!" chimed the chorus as Jen smothered a laugh—she remembered Sara's first reaction to Methuselah was similar.

Laika and Cody confronted Major Prescott.

"These animals are special. Top Secret," Cody explained. "That's why they chose you to guard them."

"We wanted the best," Laika explained. "They were going to tell you in Houston. I'm sorry to have startled you."

Major Prescott waved his hand absently. He still did not believe a word of it.

"Nah, that's okay," Major Prescott said.

He backed away from the group until his shoes were under water, but he didn't seem to notice. Laika stepped up to Patty Cake.

"Patty Cake, what did you see?" asked Laika.

"There's an Amadorian spacecraft down on an island near here and two of their soldiers are headed this way," said Patty Cake.

"They must be the ones who shot us down," said Laika.

"See Major, they won't take it out of your pay," said Cody with a grin.

"This is all like Sara's dream," said Jen with a sudden burst of inspiration.

"What dream?" asked Laika and Patty Cake together.

"You know, Sara, my best friend, had a dream the night after Methuselah told her about the Zoonauts and Animalville," said Jen. "We were all lost in a swamp and we were chased by smelly monsters. The only way we survived was because Patty Cake somehow used her 'Far See' intuition ability."

"Could it work?" Laika asked Patty Cake.

"Maybe, but first I need to have some powerful object to focus on; it has to be something I know how to use. Swamp trees won't do," said Patty Cake. "Maybe we can capture something the Aliens have."

Major Prescott suddenly noticed that he was standing in water and stepped back on the island. He shook the water from his shoes.

"Hey, talking animals are one thing, but you're not going to get me to believe that there are Aliens out there, too," Major Prescott said.

Then, as if on cue, a laser blast hit the tree above them, and the branches and leaves fell upon their heads.

"Argue later, run *now!*" said Cody grabbing Major Prescott by the arm.

Patty Cake, Laika, and the kids thrashed about wildly into the water and headed for the next island across the swamp. Major Prescott, still not convinced, ducked as another blast sliced through the trees.

"There's got to be an explanation for this," said Major Prescott to himself under his breath.

Another large branch crashed to the ground at his feet.

"This is nuts!" said Major Prescott. Despite his disbelief, he took off in a sprint and ran as fast as the rest of the Zoonauts.

CHAPTER TWENTY-ONE

SKY ABOVE AND MUD BELOW

The big heavy-lift helicopter was roaring low over the swamp and lightning forked down in the distance. Dr. Tom watched as it struck to the north of New Iberia, Louisiana. Race was flying the copter with a practiced touch. Cough Drop sat beside him with a clipboard and took notes.

"Race, when we get down, I want you to stay with the copter," said Dr. Tom.

"Roger, Skipper!" said Race the Orangutan.

Race held the control yoke with his feet. Dr. Tom decided that he'd just never be comfortable with those procedures. He tapped Cough Drop on the shoulder.

"You, too," said Dr. Tom. "Stay with the ship."

"Too, right," Cough Drop replied. "Koalas aren't built for mucking about in the swamp."

Dr. Tom reached for the intercom.

"Kongo, would you come up to the cockpit, please?" asked Dr. Tom.

"Yes, Dr. Tom?" Kongo said. He squeezed through the doorway into the cockpit.

Dr. Tom pointed to a screen on the cabin console. The computer screen displayed a shot of the bayou with lighted shapes that indicated the sunken plane with something else.

"Spysat One is over the bayou now," said Dr. Tom. "It's spotted the crash site, but what is that thing?"

"That, I fear, is an Amadorian scout ship," Kongo groaned and then snorted angrily.

"So, I am finally going to see an Amadorian," said Dr. Tom.

"Well, according to Hsing-Hsing and Cough Drop, I'm afraid they're not much to look at," said Kongo.

"How is the team holding up?" Dr. Tom asked.

Kongo rolled his eyes.

"I'll be amazed if they all don't get lost within the first five minutes," said Kongo.

In the back of the copter, the rest of the team—Ham, Mungo, and Luna— were bouncing along as the copter passed through the trailing edge of the storm. Mungo was trying out his best cowboy accent.

"All right, loosen up, people," Mungo said. "When we hit the Landing Zone [LZ], I want you to keep your eyes open and stay alert. Watch out for Charlie..."

"Charlie?" asked Ham as he looked at Luna.

Luna was licking her paws. She looked up and then glanced at Mungo.

"He lives in a world of his own," said Luna, referring to Mungo.

Mungo had switched and was now imitating one of his favorite male leads in space films.

"Is this a stand-up fight or just another bug hunt?" Mungo mimicked.

Luna looked at Ham.

"If he keeps this up, can I eat him?" asked Luna.

"No!" said Ham who looked miserable.

"Worried about Patty Cake?" Luna asked.

"Yes," replied Ham. "If anything happens to her, I'd …"

Ham paused, but seethed with anger.

"I don't know what I'd do," Ham said. "When I get my hands on whoever did this, I'll…"

Ham hadn't seen Kongo return. The huge Silverback Gorilla leaned down toward him.

"You'll do as you're told," said Kongo. "That's my daughter out there and the doctor's children with Laika. If you do anything to endanger them, I'll…"

"I wouldn't do that," Ham declared. "I love Patty Cake!"

Kongo grabbed Ham and pulled him up very close to his face.

"Love? You're just a child," said Kongo. "You should be home. You…"

Kongo broke off as he was frustrated and angry. He tried to control the rage he felt.

"My daughter is too young to be dating a teenage flying monkey," said Kongo.

"You watch," Ham said as he stared back into Kongo's angry expression. "I'll save her!"

Disgusted, Kongo turned away and stared at the wall.

Ham looked at Luna.

"Cheer up, kid," Luna said. "Romeo and Juliet had it rough at first, too."

"Shakespeare's Romeo and Juliet died," said Ham who was not comforted by Luna's reassurances.

"Oh, yeah," Luna said and shrugged. "Forget I mentioned it!"

It was early spring, dusk, and overcast with heavy clouds. All of those things combined to make the Louisiana bayou a dark and scary place. Jen and Cody were very happy to slog out of the water onto a patch of grass at the edge of the road. They were soaked to the skin and getting cold.

Across the road, there appeared to be a Rockin' Roadhouse. There was no name on the building, but neon signs flashed *Roadhouse, Eats & Drinks*. Strings of lights on poles edged the parking lot filled with pickup trucks, cars, and motorcycles. Zydeco music blared out into the dark; the smell of shrimp and catfish wafted from the kitchen and pulled them towards the Roadhouse during the last half hour.

"Civilization!" Cody cried.

Cody scrambled up and started toward the Roadhouse, but Laika and Jen tackled him to bring him down. A truck screamed past them and roared down the road at eighty miles per hour. The truck missed Cody by an inch.

"Wow," said Cody. "Thanks."

Laika looked at Cody severely.

"How many times have I told you to look both ways before you cross the road?" asked Laika.

"Got it," said Cody as he backed away from the road.

Major Prescott waded out of the muck and stopped to see the kids and Laika. Then he looked around.

"Where's the monkey," asked Major Prescott.

"Gorilla!" Jen snapped. "I thought she was with you!"

"And I thought she was with you," said Major Prescott. "Rats!"

"This is weird. It's just like Sara's dream!" said Jen. "We have to go back."

"No way!" said Major Prescott.

"But if Sara's dream is true, we need Patty Cake to get us out of this alive!" said Jen. "We…"

Just then, a way off in the swamp behind the closest trees, there came the zap and sizzle of laser fire.

"Bad idea," Major Prescott said. "We need to get you kids to safety and then I'll come back for the …the gorilla."

"But…," said Jen.

"No buts, kids," said Major Prescott. "My job is to take care of the animals. I can't do that if I have to watch you. Forget the dreams, and let's use our wits instead. Come on…I have an idea!"

Looking both ways, the Zoonauts scrambled across the road and into the parking lot. There, among parked trucks, cars, and motorcycles, the smell of the food was much stronger and almost irresistible. Major Prescott started trying the doors of the nearest trucks. The third one he tried was unlocked. He opened the door.

"Get in!" said Major Prescott.

Laika and the kids piled into the cab of the large, red pickup truck. Major Prescott popped the hood and began looking for the right wires to start the car.

"Isn't this stealing?" Cody asked leaning out of the cab.

"That's what I was gonna ask," interrupted a huge, bearded man in greasy dungarees and a leather jacket.

Major Prescott turned to look at the man who was holding a pool cue like a club.

"US Government," said Major Prescott as he swallowed hard. "We need this truck."

"You a cop?" asked the man.

"US Air Force," replied Major Prescott.

"What's the Air Force need with a truck?" asked the man.

Laika stuck his head out of the cab.

"Actually, we're borrowing it," said Laika. "As a military officer, the Major has the right to commandeer civilian transport in times of war."

The man in the greasy dungarees looked at Laika and his eyes widened in disbelief.

"A talking dog? Cool!" the man said as he scratched his woolly head. "You mean those enemies of ours are right here in Louisiana?"

At that moment, a laser blast shot out of the swamp and hit the Roadhouse's highway sign, which fell down in a crash of sparks.

"Sorry, I asked," said the man as he ran for cover. "It ain't my truck anyhow."

The truck engine roared to life and Major Prescott slammed the hood. He jumped into the cab of the truck and drove out of the gravel lot onto the road.

Moments later, Fishwick and Kornblend came up out of the swamp. Fishwick was consulting the life detector while Kornblend looked around for something else to shoot with his laser. Suddenly, Kornblend spotted the Roadhouse.

"Outstanding!" said Kornblend.

"Leave it alone," said Fishwick. "I'm getting confusing readings. There are a lot of Earthlings in there and some more in that direction."

Fishwick gestured to Kornblend in the direction of the red pickup truck as the lights disappeared down the highway.

"Where are the most Earthlings?" asked Kornblend.

"In the building," Fishwick replied.

"All right then," Kornblend growled as he shifted into his action figure mode. He held the laser high across his chest and marched toward the Roadhouse.

"Yippee, Ki-Yay!" shouted Kornblend.

Fishwick shrugged and followed his fellow Amadorian straight into trouble.

As Fishwick and Kornblend stepped into the Roadhouse, everything stopped.

Fifty or sixty bikers, oil field workers, and fisherman with their girlfriends stared at the two dragons. Then Kornblend, seized by the odors of cooking fish, stalked to the fryer and emptied the contents, grease and all, into his mouth.

"Mmmmmm," said Kornblend.

"Who's gone der pay for dat fish, you big ugly lizard, you?" asked the Cajun cook who stepped up to Kornblend with his fists clenched.

Kornblend looked at him and let out a huge belch that smelled of fish and grease. It smelled so horrible when mixed with the gas that normally comes from the stomach of an Amadorian that the Cajun cook staggered backwards; then he leaned into a roadhouse right and hit Kornblend as hard as he could in the schnoz. Kornblend just looked at the cook.

"No good can come of this," Fishwick said shaking his head.

Then Kornblend raised his laser and blew the roof off the building; all of the humans ran in the opposite directions away from the demolished building.

Major Prescott, the kids and Laika—all squeezed into the front seat of the pickup—tore down the road at high speed in an effort to make a temporary getaway. It was disturbing how easily the Amadorians were able to follow them. It was almost as if they could read their minds.

"How do we get back to Patty Cake?" Jen asked.

"First, I leave you kids with the cops in the nearest town, then that dog and I..." said Major Prescott as he worked out his plan as he spoke it aloud.

"My name is Laika," said Laika.

"Sorry," said Major Prescott. "Then we retrace our steps. Simple, right? Let's go, Laika!"

"Sounds like a plan, but there may be a problem," said Cody as he looked into the rearview mirror.

Major Prescott looked in the rearview mirror, too. There was a big tricycle motorcycle coming up behind them fast. Fishwick piloted and Kornblend rode behind him with his laser sticking up between the two Amadorians. Both were now wearing biker vests over their armor.

"They are faster than we are and they've got that blasted laser gun," said Major Prescott slamming his fist angrily on the dashboard.

"Well, floor it!" Jen shouted.

Major Prescott pushed the gas pedal to the floor. The red pickup shot down the darkened highway well over the speed limit. Fortunately, they were on official government business.

Fishwick sat hunched over the handlebars of the tricycle and tried to ignore the wind screaming past his snout. He blew a bug out of his nasal flaps.

"This Earth machine isn't safe!" he shouted.

"Faster! Faster!" said Kornblend who was having entirely too much fun. "This is exciting and we're going to be heroes. I'm your worst nightmare, Zoonauts!"

"Any faster and we'll be dead heroes!" groaned Fishwick.

Kornblend fired his laser weapon and the shot went off so close to Fishwick's head that he thought he'd been hit.

"Yahhhh!" cried Fishwick.

"What?" asked Kornblend.

"You hit me!" shouted Fishwick.

"Did not!" said Kornblend. "Don't be such an egg. Any true action hero would never say that!"

"I am no Earth action figure," said Fishwick. He was furious at this point. "You are no Earth action figure! Now shoot that vehicle!"

The first laser shot missed its target and went into the forest. The next shot slugged a hole in the highway alongside the speeding red pickup truck.

"That was too close," said Major Prescott.

"Perhaps there's something I can do," said Laika.

Laika wriggled through the cab window and into the bed of the pickup truck. He looked over the tailgate. The motor-trike was getting closer. Kornblend fired again. This time the shot was right on target, but a glistening force bubble appeared to deflect and scatter the laser light beam.

"I hit it," said Kornblend with his eyes narrowed. "How'd they do that? Do Earth speeders have force fields?"

"It's the dog. The one we want," cried Fishwick. "He's doing it. Shoot again!"

Kornblend fired again.

In the bed of the red pickup, Laika saw the laser glow again and he concentrated. A silver force bubble formed around the rear of the red pickup just as the laser light hit it, and the laser light beam scattered again.

"That was cool!" exclaimed Jen and Cody looking through the rear window of the cab. "Yeah! Laika!"

"Yeah, cool," said Jen punching her brother's arm. "But how long can he keep it up?"

In the back bed of the truck, Laika realized that Jen was right. There were only so many times he could cast that force bubble before his energy was spent.

In the cab, Major Prescott concentrated on the road ahead. Suddenly, brilliant searchlights stabbed shafts of light through the forest and bathed the road in light.

"Now, what?" questioned Major Prescott out loud.

More searchlights struck the vehicle and the air suddenly filled with flying debris and a huge *"whooosh"* of air.

"We're trapped!" yelled Major Prescott as he jammed on the brakes.

The pickup went skidding to a stop as a glowing craft dropped onto the road in front of them. Major Prescott, Jen, and Cody were frozen in their seats as they shielded their eyes with the backs of their hands while they tried to see against the glaring light. Then, Cody recognized the craft in front of them.

"Well, I'll be…," said Cody.

"We're saved," said Jen with relief.

"Saved?" Major Prescott asked.

The lights shifted so that they could see a big heavy-lift helicopter on the road in front of them with Kongo standing in the open doorway.

"It's an Earth ship!" Kornblend screamed as he and Fishwick on their motor-trike also spotted the craft. "Stop this thing!"

"Sure! How?" asked Fishwick who banged on the handlebars since he had no idea where the brakes were.

"Turn it!" shouted Kornblend.

Fishwick turned the handlebars.

Now every child knows that if you're riding a tricycle fast and you turn the handlebars that you're going to have an accident, but apparently they didn't have tricycles on Amador. The front wheel of the motor-trike suddenly locked and launched its riders cart-wheeling end-over-end into the dark swamp.

"Yaaaaaaaaahhh!" screamed Kornblend.

For a moment there was silence and then a huge splash in the swamp.

"This is all your fault!" screamed Fishwick.

Back on the road, Dr. Tom jumped out of the helicopter and ran to embrace his children as Race and Cough Drop powered down the craft. Ham, Mungo, and Luna peered into the darkness outside the craft and waited for their eyes to adjust to the inky blackness of the bayou. Kongo bounded past them with Dr. Tom.

"Wow, am I glad to see you," said Dr. Tom. "Are you all right?"

"We're okay, Dad," said Cody. "Chill out! Uh-oh!"

Major Prescott stood staring in shocked surprise at Kongo who was looking around for Patty Cake.

"Where's my daughter?" asked Kongo as he stepped up to Laika.

"Now don't get upset, old friend," said Laika.

"Patty Cake!" Kongo screamed. He was a gorilla about to lose his temper. "Where is she?"

Kongo began to pound the road leaving holes in the asphalt. The others watched nervously.

"I'll bring her back," said Ham. He stepped gallantly out of the helicopter.

"Not a word from you," said Kongo as he turned to warn Ham before turning to face Major Prescott.

"And who are you?" asked Kongo.

"I'm Major Davis Prescott," said Major Prescott. "I'm your new security officer, I guess."

"You guess?" said Kongo. "You're not doing a very good job, are you Major?"

Then the Major lost his temper.

"Nobody told me I'd be working with talking animals!" Major Prescott exclaimed. "Nobody told me I'd be shot down by Aliens! Nobody said anything about a swamp!"

Kongo stopped. He blinked at the irrational outburst of Major Prescott. Then his hands began to curl into fists. Dr. Tom Stroud knew that one swing of Kongo's fist could send poor Major Prescott flying over the trees.

"Kongo!" shouted Dr. Tom.

Kongo, frozen with anger, turned and looked at Dr. Tom.

"Kongo, this isn't helping," said Dr. Tom.

Kongo's anger suddenly fell away as he returned to reason.

"No, of course not," said Kongo. "You're absolutely right! What do we do?"

"I know what I am doing," said Ham stomping impatiently from foot-to-foot. "I'm gonna find Patty Cake."

With a few bouncing steps, Ham lofted into the air and disappeared into the darkness.

"Ham!" cried Dr. Tom. "Come back here!"

"How'd he do that?" asked Major Prescott as he stared after the flying chimpanzee.

"That boy is impossible," replied Kongo shaking his head.

"This whole business is impossible!" said Major Prescott.

Kongo turned to look at the bedraggled officer in his ruined uniform. Despite his confusion, Major Prescott held himself like a soldier.

"Major, my apologies," said Kongo. "I know you are trying to help my daughter and the others."

"We'll find your daughter, sir!" said Major Prescott.

"Where are Mungo and Luna?" asked Dr. Tom.

"They went after the Amadorians," said Cough Drop and Race.

"I tried to stop them, but…," said Laika with a very tired shrug.

Dr. Tom shook his head.

"That does it," said Dr. Tom. "Now we have four lost animals. Nobody else leaves—we all stay together. Major, here is a Spysat map of the crash site. Can you get us back to where your plane went down?"

"I think so," said Major Prescott. He studied the map and traced the path back to the downed craft.

Kongo smiled at Dr. Tom and shook his head.

"Didn't I say it?" said Kongo. "All of them, lost, within the first five minutes!"

CHAPTER TWENTY-TWO

THE HUNT FOR PATTY CAKE

The springs on the red pickup truck were noticeably lower as Kongo, Laika, and the Stroud children crowded into the back of the truck with Race and Cough Drop. Major Prescott and Dr. Tom were in the cab. Major Prescott gripped the wheel as if he was trying to find something real to hang onto.

"Cheer up, Major!" said Dr. Tom. "You'll get used to it!"

"I doubt it," said Major Prescott with a pause. "Are there many more of these…?"

"Zoonauts," said Dr. Tom. "We call them 'Zoonauts,' but their exact numbers are classified."

"Holy moly!" replied Major Prescott.

"Yeah," said Dr. Tom. "That was my first reaction, too!"

Dr. Tom glanced through the back window at Kongo with his huge worried face staring out at the swamp along the highway.

In another part of the swamp, the storm had left the reflection of a bright moon glistening on the water. Mungo and Luna made their way, with Mungo fluttering from branch to branch. Mungo flapped his wings up to the top of a lightening-split stump and craned his neck about.

"I can't see them," Mungo said.

"Well, I can smell them," said Luna. "They're about one hundred yards ahead."

Mungo moved down to perch on a vine that began to move. He realized it was a snake when the large reptile turned its head to glance back toward Mungo.

"Awwwk!" cried Mungo. "Snakes! I hate snakes!"

Mungo quickly flew to a safer branch as the snake glided into the water.

"Cute," muttered Luna.

"Be careful," Mungo warned in a whisper. "This place is dangerous."

"Dangerous?" said Luna sitting smugly on a log. "I come from a long, proud line of hunting cats."

Then an eye opened on the log, which was actually an alligator.

"Masters of the wilderness...experts in stealth and surprise," chirped Mungo. He flapped his wings in agitation. "Luna!"

The alligator opened its mouth and gobbled up Luna and then dove under the water. Mungo freaked out and beat his wings frantically. He hovered over the spot where Luna had disappeared.

"May Day! May Day!" cried Mungo. "Officer down! Medic! Call the US Coast Guard!"

Nothing came from the depths of the swamp except a few bubbles.

Beneath the bayou, as the alligator sank to the bottom, Luna "ghosted out" through the side of the beast and paddled frantically upward. She broke the surface of the swampy waters and pulled herself up on a real log.

"You're lucky you can do that!" said Mungo with relief. "You look like a drowned muskrat."

"Shut up," said Luna sputtering. She looked more like a wet toilet brush.

"So which way now?" asked Mungo.

"I think this way," Luna said. "Not sure!"

Luna lifted her nose up to sniff and then sneezed.

"Wha-choo!" sneezed Luna exasperated.

"Bless you," said Mungo.

"I've got mud up my nose."

Luna stalked off and Mungo flitted after her. They didn't notice Ham flying overhead looking for Patty Cake.

Ham watched the moonlit swamp intently as he wove back and forth in the air. He quartered confusing patches of water and trees in a grid search pattern with the hope he hadn't drifted off course. He could fly, but he wasn't good at it. Then he spotted the Amadorian ship on a small island.

"Excellent!" said Ham. He spiraled down to a landing next to the football-shaped ship. The door was open and a red light spilled out. Ham took a deep breath and remembered what had happened to the animals— Chuma and Bandit—after they were captured by the Aliens. He peeked carefully inside the craft.

"Great," Patty Cake grumped. "Out of one cage and then into another."

"Patty Cake!" said Ham. He leaned against the cage bars where she languished inside. There appeared to be no doors.

"Oh!" exclaimed Patty Cake.

The startled Patty Cake banged her head on the top of the cage. She ran to the bars and kissed Ham through the steel rods.

Embarrassed, each drew back from one another.

"Oh! I, uh…I'm glad to see you," Patty Cake said.

"Yeah, heh heh, me too!" said Ham. He grinned like a fool after he finally got a kiss from Patty Cake. He was in heaven!

"Is my Dad here?" asked Patty Cake.

"Where?" asked Ham. Startled, Ham jumped backward with the sudden realization that Kongo might be behind him.

"Oh, you mean…No…I came alone," said Ham. "Let's get you out of there. Can you use your powers on the door?"

"There is no door," said Patty Cake. "They welded me in and the bars are too strong."

"I've got an idea," Ham said. "Don't go away."

Patty Cake shrugged and then turned away and shook the bars.

"Where would I go?" she asked.

Suddenly she heard a click and an electronic sound powering up. Ham's voice came from behind her.

"Duck!" ordered Ham.

Patty Cake turned back and threw herself to the bottom of her cage as she saw Ham holding a laser gun that was too heavy for his grasp.

"Noooooo!" exclaimed Patty Cake with her hands over her eyes. Ham fired the gun.

Patty Cake looked up to see the bars of her cage melt off at different lengths.

"Well, that was good," she remarked with uncertainty.

"Come on," said Ham.

They paused in the doorway of the craft and peered into the swamp. It looked peaceful enough until they heard the Amadorian voices bellowing in the distance.

"We still have to get the dog," said Fishwick to Kornblend.

"Why?" asked Kornblend. "We got the monkey."

"Gorilla," said Fishwick. "Because they want the dog. Remember? Do you want to be luggage?"

Ham and Patty Cake looked at each other.

"Now I've got an idea," Patty Cake said. "There might be something to Sara's crazy dream after all."

Some distance away, Fishwick and Kornblend slogged through the swamp toward their football-shaped craft. Fishwick stopped and his nasal slots popped with irritation.

"What is that disgusting smell?" asked Fishwick. "What have you been eating?"

"Nothing," replied Kornblend. "It isn't me! It's this swamp. It's gross!"

"The Amadorian Codex says…" started Fishwick.

"Enough of the Amadorian Codex," Kornblend groaned. "I'm sick of hearing about it and I am sick of you!"

"I'm going to request another sidekick," Fishwick complained.

Just then, headlights appeared in the swamp. Kornblend tapped Fishwick on the shoulder and practically knocked him over.

"What?" asked Fishwick.

"Look!" said Kornblend.

"This could be good," Fishwick said. He rubbed his snout thoughtfully as they peered at the headlights moving through the swamp.

Hunt for Patty Cake

CHAPTER TWENTY-THREE

NOSE TO NOSE

The truck pulled up to the dock at the end of the road and stopped. Major Prescott turned off the lights. Then Prescott and Dr. Tom got out of the pickup truck to look around with their flashlights. Jen, Cody, Laika, and Kongo tumbled out of the back of the truck flatbed.

"Laika, can you find their ship from here?" Dr. Tom asked. He found Laika on the dock sniffing the air.

"I think so, but we're going to get wet," replied Laika. "Here goes!"

Laika trotted back to the shore along the tangled tree roots to the end of the marshland before diving in. Laika swam and led Dr. Tom and Major Prescott through the waters. Kongo brought up the rear with both Cody and Jen riding on his mighty shoulders. The search party moved across the murky waters as Major Prescott waved his flashlight across the swamp with more than a little concern.

"What about alligators?" asked Major Prescott.

"I'll smell them before we see them," Kongo growled.

"Cool," said Cody.

"Yeah, cool!" said Major Prescott. He wasn't thoroughly convinced.

After wading about two hundred yards and stepping more than once on things that slithered out from under their feet, Laika led them up onto a little island.

"Do you smell that?" asked Laika. He stopped in his tracks.

"Alligators?" asked Major Prescott.

"Amadorians! Close!" Laika said. Kongo moved up to join him at the front of the group.

"Very close!" Kongo said.

"How do you know they are Amadorians?" asked Jen.

"Because I know all of the smells of the swamp," Kongo said. "That smell is not one of them."

"It's rancid," added Laika. "Like dirty old socks and garbage. Yes, they are close."

"Too close," Cody exclaimed. Fishwick and Kornblend stepped out of the bushes, battle ready; each brandished a laser.

"You try riding around in one of our ships for a few weeks and see how you smell," Fishwick snarled at Laika. "And you will!"

"Up against the wall, feet back, and spread 'em," said Kornblend caught in the drama of his own world.

Fishwick looked at him trying not to explode.

"Will you *puleeeease* stop doing that?" Fishwick demanded. "He watches too much television."

"Awl-right!" Kornblend said grumpily.

"Where's my daughter?" demanded Kongo. He was rapidly losing patience.

"Ah, the other gorilla," said Fishwick. "Yes, well, we'll give her back if we can have the dog!"

"What?" asked Kongo.

"Forget it," Dr. Tom cried. "The US Government doesn't bargain with kidnappers."

"Or Aliens!" Jen added.

"You would make a tasty snack, little girl!" Kornblend said. Next, he turned his laser gun on Jen.

"Uh, yeah?" Major Prescott added.

Major Prescott contemplated whether to reach for his gun, but the two huge lasers in the hands of the Aliens decided the issue for him. Laika stepped forward.

"No!" said Laika. "I'll go. If, you give back Patty Cake."

Kongo looked stricken, not knowing what to do.

"Let me do this, old friend," said Laika to Kongo.

Their plan was working as Fishwick and Kornblend grinned at one another. Medals would be theirs and another stripe for each. What they didn't see behind them, however, was that their ship was approaching silently through the darkness.

Kongo and Major Prescott had seen it.

"That boy is impossible!" Kongo muttered referring to Ham.

Through the cockpit windshield of the Amadorian spacecraft, Ham and Patty Cake were watching as the ship's levers moved on autopilot.

"How do you do that?" asked Ham.

"I just imagine where I want the ship to be. Then it goes there—just like in Sara's dream, I guess," said Patty Cake. "I don't know how it works."

"Well, I know how this works," Ham said as he grabbed a microphone and moved a lever around to where he wanted it.

The ship was now hovering right behind the Amadorians with its big laser cannons pointing directly at them.

"Time's up," Fishwick announced. "What do you say?"

"Drop the irons and reach for the sky?" boomed Ham on the Alien spacecraft's loudspeaker.

A startled Fishwick and Kornblend did just that and then turned to see their own ship covering them with lethal intent.

"Wow!" said Kornblend shaking his head in amazement. "These Earth creatures are tough."

"Shut up, luggage face!" hissed Fishwick.

"These are some funky animals!" said Major Prescott. He was clearly impressed with Ham and Patty Cake.

"Zoonauts, Major!" Kongo corrected. "What shall we do with these evil doers, Dr. Tom?"

"Let us go, or there'll be an invasion fleet here in twenty minutes," said Fishwick as he swished his tail about angrily.

"There will?" said Kornblend who looked surprised.

"Just once, read the updates we get from headquarters," said Fishwick. He shook his head before turning to explain his partner's ineptitude to Dr. Tom and Major Prescott. "You see what I have to work with here?"

"An invasion fleet?" asked Kornblend.

"Yes, in ten minutes," said Fishwick. "Big fleet. Lots of ships. Boom! Boom! Boom!"

"He's bluffing," said Major Prescott. Major Prescott and Dr. Tom looked at one another.

"Maybe," said Dr. Tom. "I can't risk starting an interplanetary war just to find out."

Dr. Tom scrutinized the two oversized lizards.

"All right," Dr. Tom said. "We'll let you go this time, but stay off this planet! Or the next time, you won't be so lucky."

"Until next time!" said Kornblend shaking his fist. "It ain't over 'til we say it's over."

"Enough!" said Fishwick.

Ten minutes later, both the humans and Zoonauts watched as the Amadorian ship streaked into the night sky.

"What was that all about? 'Luggage?'" Major Prescott asked Cody.

"Who knows?" replied Cody. "You know the Amadorians don't seem too bright to me. Do you think they're all like that?"

"Hmmm. Why didn't they just blast us when they got their ship back?" Major Prescott asked.

"Maybe they were under orders not to," said Dr. Tom.

"Or maybe their targeting computer doesn't work properly," said Ham smiling as he passed a handful of computer chips to Major Prescott.

"I'll be darned," said Major Prescott.

"What did we miss?" asked Mungo. He and a bedraggled Luna shuffled into the light where Ham was standing close to Patty Cake who had her arms around Kongo.

Dr. Tom shrugged as he looked at Major Prescott.

"Apparently everything," Laika said.

Glancing up at Kongo, Patty Cake asked, "Can we go home now? I want to thank Sara for her dream. I couldn't have saved all of you any other way."

"I think that is an excellent idea," Kongo replied.

"I'm glad that's over," said Major Prescott looking up at the Amadorian spacecraft as it disappeared like a star in the sky.

"Oh, they'll be back," said Dr. Tom.

"Yeah," said Laika. "It's just a matter of time; let's head on home now as I would like to see my new son and Heisler."

CHAPTER TWENTY-FOUR

LUCKY BRAVO

The adventurers arrived home by midnight, and all returned to the "normal" life at Animalville. Sara became an Honorary Zoonaut. Of course, Methuselah was credited with sharing the secret of Animalville with Sara. Sara's first dream had already proved to be prophetic, true, and helpful.

Her dream of the dangerous plants had yet to become a reality. Zoonauts encourage children and adults to record their dreams as Sara does because one day the dreams may prove to be important. It is often said a goal is a dream with a deadline. Sara keeps a notepad by her bed.

So, pay close attention to your dreams as they can take you to places you might not otherwise ever go.

The next few days, upon the Zoonauts' return to Animalville, US Air Force officers and investigators debriefed the team. It was tedious as usual. Major Prescott got a tour of Animalville to meet all the Zoonauts. Slowly, he adjusted to life in Animalville, but, it will likely take a while.

The Amadorians have been quiet in the weeks that followed their visit. There hasn't even been one of their scout ships sighted in orbit over

Animalville, so maybe they are planning their next mission to avoid the alternative—to become Tre-Pok's luggage.

Dr. Tom, like many, believe the Amadorians will return and have not yet given up their conquest of Earth and the Zoonauts. Whatever their plans, the Zoonauts will be here to meet their challenge.

The Zoonauts, Cody, Jen, and Sara, with the special creatures of Animalville, are, and will remain, Earth's first line of defense.

This battle between Amador and Earth has drawn to an end, but the conflict is not over. There will be many new and exciting adventures with and without the Amadorians, led by the unique and special superheroes, the Zoonauts!

~THE END~

Coming in 2016
Zoonauts: Adventures in China
Visit the Zoonauts online at www.zoonauts.com

APPENDIX A

SPACE MILESTONE TIME LINE

- In **1944**, Germany developed a liquid fuel rocket called V-2. Instead of using it in space, the Germans shot explosive warheads at Great Britain but still lost the war. The United States brought back many V-2 rockets.

- In **1945**, White Sands Proving Ground, New Mexico, was opened for rocket research.

- In **1946**, a US-launched V-22 rocket carried a spectrograph 34 miles high to study the sun.

- In **1947**, a US jet plane broke the sound barrier for the first time piloted by Captain Chuck Yeager.

- In **1949**, a rocket test ground launch was set up at Cape Canaveral Fla. At White Sands NM, Missile Base, the first two-stage rocket flew up 240 miles.

- In **1955**, the United States began the Vanguard Project for launching artificial satellites.

- In **1957**, Russia (formerly the Soviet Union) launched its first artificial satellite, Sputnik I, and launched a second satellite carrying a live dog, **Laika**.

- In **1958**, the first US Vanguard satellite went into orbit.

- In **1959**, the Russians put a satellite (Lunik) in orbit around the sun and crash-landed a rocket (Lunik II) on the moon. Lunik III then photographed the dark side of the moon.

- Also in **1959**, **Miss Baker**, a squirrel monkey who was called America's "First Lady in Space," flew into space on a US Jupiter rocket and returned safely to Earth.

- In **1960**, Echo, the first communications satellite, was launched by the United States.

- In **1961**, Russian Cosmonauts Yuri Gagarin and German Titov became the first two humans to orbit Earth.

- Also in **1961**, **Ham**, a chimpanzee, paved the way for Alan Shepard and Virgil "Gus" Grissom to become the first and second Mercury astronauts in suborbital flights. They splashed down in the Atlantic.

- In **1962**, the US Mariner Spacecraft reached Venus. John Glenn became the first American to orbit Earth. The Telestar Communications Satellite was launched. American Astronaut Scott Carpenter and Wally Schirra orbited Earth.

- In **1963**, Russian Valentine Tereshkova-Nikolayeva became the first woman in space.

- In **1964**, the US Ranger 7 probe took 4,316 pictures of the moon.

- In **1965**, Cosmonaut Aleksi Leonov took the first spacewalk. US Astronauts Virgil Grissom and John Young rode the first two-man Gemini capsule. The Mariner IV Spacecraft reached Mars.

- In **1966**, the Russian probe Luna X became the first to orbit the moon.

- In **1967**, Americans Virgil "Gus" Grissom, Ed White, and Roger Chafee died in the Apollo I spacecraft fire. Surveyor III landed safely on the moon and took pictures and soil samples. The American Mariner V and Russian Venera 4 probes visited Venus. Neil Armstrong became the first human to walk on the moon and famously said, "One giant step for man, one giant leap for mankind."

- In **1971**, Salyut I, the first space station for Russia, went into orbit. The Mars 3 probe landed on Mars.

- In **1972**, Probe Pioneer 10 launched. It was the first human object to leave the solar system.

- In **1973**, American Skylab Space Station went into orbit...and stayed there until 1979.

- In **1975**, Russian Cosmonauts and American Astronauts carried out Apollo-Soyuz as the first Russian-US joint mission.

- In **1976**, the space probes Viking 1 and Viking 2 soft-landed on Mars and began sending back pictures.

- In **1977**, the long-distance probes, Voyager 1 and Voyager 2, were launched to study Jupiter and the outer planets. They carried messages of friendship, recordings of Earth sounds, and music to introduce us to any Aliens they encountered. Earlier, Pioneers 10 and 11 had small metal plaques identifying their origin for any spacefarers that might find them.

- In **1979**, Voyager 1 discovered a ring around Jupiter. The Skylab 1 space station fell back to Earth, landing in the Australian desert.

- In **1980**, Voyager 1 and 2 flew by the planet Saturn and discovered two moons.

- In **1981**, Space Shuttle Columbia made its first flight, and in 1982, it made four more flights.

- In **1983**, Space Shuttle Challenger made three flights and a fourth in 1984. Sally K. Ride was America's first woman in space.

- In **1985**, the Space Shuttle Challenger blew apart seventy-three seconds after launch, killing six astronauts and Teacher S. Christa McAuliffe. This disaster almost ended the American space program.

- In **1986**, Mir (Peace) went into operation becoming the first permanently manned space station.

- In **1989**, Voyager 2 left our solar system to teach any extraterrestrials about us. NASA placed ambitious messages about our world on both Voyager 1 and 2. The Voyager greeting, recorded on a twelve-inch, gold-plated phonograph, contains sounds and images of Earth's life and cultures. A committee, chaired by Carl Sagan, picked the contents for NASA.

- In **1990**, Voyager 1 looked back from Deep Space and took the first photo of our Solar System. The Magellan spacecraft began mapping the surface of Venus using radar equipment. The Space Shuttle Discovery deployed the Hubble Telescope.

- In **1991**, the probe Galileo flew through the Asteroid Belt.

- In **1992**, The Space Shuttle Endeavor was launched on her maiden voyage. Mae Jemison became the first African-American woman in space.

- In **1993**, The Space Shuttle Endeavor made the first servicing mission of the Hubble Telescope.

- In **1994**, Sergei Krikalev became the first Russian cosmonaut to fly on a Space Shuttle.

- In **1995,** Eileen Collins became the first female Shuttle pilot.

- In **1996,** The Galileo probe began transmitting data on Jupiter (December 1995).

- In **1997,** The Mars Pathfinder arrived on Mars and later began transmitting images.

- In **1998,** John Glenn became the oldest man in space.

- In **1999,** Eileen Collins became the first female Space Shuttle Commander.

- In **2000,** the US Near-Earth Asteroid Rendezvous (NEAR) Spacecraft began transmitting images of Eros.

- In **2001,** NEAR landed on the surface of EROS; American Dennis Tito became the first tourist in space after paying the Russian Space Program $20,000,000.

- In **2003,** the Space Shuttle Columbia broke apart on reentry into the Earth's atmosphere over Central Texas. NASA warned about contaminated debris. The Department of Homeland Security reported there was no sign of terrorism.

- In **2004,** achieving a feat unparalleled in history, NASA successfully landed two mobile geology labs, Spirit and Opportunity, on the surface of Mars.

- In **2005,** NASA's Earth-observing "eyes in the sky," included Earth-orbiting satellites, aircraft, and the International Space Station; these "eyes in the sky" provided detailed images of the flooding and devastation by Hurricanes Katrina and Rita. NASA worked to ensure the Department of Homeland Security and FEMA received the best information available to aid the rescue and recovery effort.

- In **2006,** NASA launched the spaceship New Horizons on the first mission to Pluto, Pluto's moon Charon, and the Kuiper Belt.

- In **2007,** NASA successfully launched four new space science missions designed to improve our understanding of solar processes, the Earth, and the history of the solar system.

- In **2008,** NASA successfully launched six new space and Earth science missions designed to improve our understanding of solar processes, Earth, the universe, and the history of the solar system.

- In **2009,** NASA launched the Wide-Field Infrared Survey Explorer (WISE) spacecraft. By the end of its six-month mission, WISE acquired nearly 1,500,000 images covering the entire sky that will be studied for years to come to answer fundamental questions about the origins of planets, stars, and galaxies and reveal new information about the composition of near Earth objects and asteroids.

- In **2010,** NASA's Hubble Space Telescope's new infrared camera, the Wide Field Camera 3 (WFC3), broke the distance limit for galaxies and uncovered a primordial population of compact and ultrablue galaxies that have never been seen before. Hubble is a powerful "time machine" that allows astronomers to see the most distant galaxies as they were thirteen billion years ago.

- In **2011,** NASA began developing a heavy-lift rocket for the human exploration of deep space and helped foster a new era of commercial spaceflight and breakthroughs in technology. Utilizing a newly completed Space Station, major discoveries were made about the universe that will benefit our lives here on Earth.

- In **2013,** NASA helped US commercial companies transform access to low-Earth orbit and the International Space Station; one of the agency's spacecrafts was confirmed to have reached Interstellar Space. Engineers moved ahead to develop technologies that will carry out the first astronaut mission to an asteroid and eventually to Mars.

- In 2014, Gioia Massa who leads the Veggie science team-has been working on the veggie project for years. This team has been experimenting with plants and gardening aboard the Russian space station Mir and NASA's space shuttle. They are very close to resolving gardening problems in a weightless environment.

- In 2015, on September 28th NASA reported there was water on Mars and announced their findings suggest "it would be possible for there to be life today on Mars," according to NASA Mission Chief John Grunsfield. On Mars, each day is 40 minutes longer-and each year has 687 days, compared to 365 on earth.

APPENDIX B

DAVID SIMONS

BIOGRAPHY

"We are not superior to animals, but different; we have much to teach each other."

~ David Simons

David Simons is the creator of the *Zoonauts* children's series for young adults. Simons was inspired as a young adult by Animal Behaviorist Frank Buck. A physical, face-to-face meeting at the Central Park Zoo with the world famous Silverback Gorilla Patty Cake became the inspiration for the Zoonauts Series.

Simons was born in New York City in Manhattan and served in the Merchant Marines and traveled to many countries around the world. He also served as a medic in the US Army. He later had a successful career in the real estate industry. He was also partners in the music production industry with Cathy Lynn, a successful composer.

Simons developed a promotional concept around Patty Cake, a Silverback Gorilla, and one of the world's most famous primates who was born in the Central Park Zoo and later moved to larger accommodations in the Bronx Zoo. Patty Cake became Simon's inspiration for the *Zoonauts* series.

Simons has been a lifelong resident of Manhattan, New York, and has one son, Cody.

APPENDIX C

AUTHOR

RICHARD MUELLER

BIOGRAPHY

Richard Mueller is author of *Jernigan's Egg*, *Time Machine 24*, and *Ghostbusters: The Supernatural Spectacular*. He has written scripts for *Dogfights*, *Legend of the Dragon*, *Matrimony Con Hijos*, *Kong the Animated Series*, *Stargate: Infinity*, *Milo's Great Adventure*, *Buzz Lightyear of Star Command*, *Robocop: Alpha Commando*, *Roswell Conspiracies: Aliens, Myths and Legends*, *Ghostbusters*, *Captain Simian & The Space Monkeys*, *Wing Commander Academy*, *Hypernauts*, *X-Men*, *Exosquad*, *Captain Planet and the Planeteers*, *Conan: The Adventurer*, *Land of the Lost*, *Batman: The Animated Series*, *Super Dave: Daredevil for Hire*, *The Real Ghostbusters*, *Attack of the Killer Tomatoes*, *Tiny Toon Adventures*, *Married with Children*, *Police Academy: The Series*, *C.O.P.S.*, *Starcom: The US Space Force*, *Dinosaucers*, *Spiral Zone*, *Adventures of the Gummi Bears*, *Milo's Great Adventure*, *Buzz Lightyear of Star Command*, *Motorcop*, *X-Men*, *Land of the Lost*, *Attack of the Killer Tomatoes*, and *Married with Children*. He lives in Los Angeles.

APPENDIX D

ILLUSTRATOR

EDIGIO VICTOR DAL CHELE

BIOGRAPHY

Edigio Victor Dal Chele is known for his role in directing animated programs for film and television to include: *Fright On!, Monster High: Fright On!, My Little Pony: The Princess Promenade, My Little Pony: A Very Minty Christmas, Static Shock, Go–Bots. Butt-Ugly Martians, Robo-Cop: Alpha Commando, Extreme Ghostbusters, and Skeleton Warriors.* He has credits as art director in *Fright On!, Exosquad, and The Karate Kid.* He was also producer *of Robo-Cop: Alpha Commando, Skeleton Warriors, and Darkstalkers.* As a writer, he has credits in *Bravestar. Dal Chele has more than forty-three credits as an art department animator and is also known for his work in God, the Devil and Bob, Scooby Doo, The Alien Invaders, All Dogs Christmas, He-Man & The Masters of the Universe, Fat Albert, and Shazam.*

He lives in Los Angeles.

APPENDIX E

LIST OF ILLUSTRATIONS
BY EDIGIO VICTOR DAL CHELE

APPENDIX F

MAP OF ANIMALVILLE

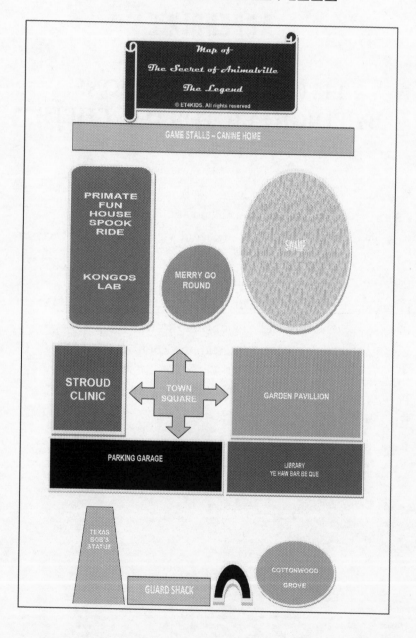

APPENDIX G

(Alphabetically)
MAIN CHARACTERS

Biff the Mouse — A Zoonaut who after being struck by the yellow light has the ability to type using his feet on a the typewriter keyboard to write reports; later, he becomes an excellent stenographer and dances from key-to-key on an electric typewriter and computer keyboard.

Cody Stroud — The son of Dr. Tom and Dr. Angie Stroud; younger and only brother to Jennifer Stroud. Cody plays an important role in the rescue of the pandas Ling-Ling and Hsing-Hsing from Tibet.

Cough Drop the Koala —A Zoonaut from Australia, his special power is creating light and darkness.

Dr. Angie Stroud — Jenny and Cody's mother who maintains a fully equipped veterinary hospital complete with a psychic research unit in Animalville. She loves all animals and was recruited (with her newlywed husband, Dr. Tom Stroud) to join Animalville right after completion of veterinary graduate school.

Dr. Brooks Wagoner, NASA — An African-American born in Senegal, Africa. He was assigned as administrator to the Animal Unit. Dr. Brooks Wagoner protects the secrets of Animalville. Mostly, he worries about how to account for everything to the US Government in Washington, DC., without revealing the Zoonauts activities. Annually, he faces the challenge of securing government funding for the operations of Animalville.

Dr. Tom Stroud— Jenny and Cody's father and the veterinarian who leads the Zoonauts and looks after them with his wife, Dr. Angie Stroud. Together, they maintain a fully equipped veterinary hospital complete with a psychic research unit in Animalville. He was recruited (with his newlywed spouse) Dr. Angie Stroud to join Animalville right after completion of veterinary graduate school.

Fishwick — One of two Amadorian Aliens (who look like dragons) whose mission is to bring back Laika the Russian Dog alive to Amador

Ham the Chimpanzee—A Zoonaut who helps rescue Patty Cake from the Amadorians. His special talent is his ability to fly and levitate.

Hsing-Hsing the Panda — A Chinese Panda whose special talent is the ability to read Amadorian minds and memories. He can absorb Amadorian experiences, fears, gossip, and legends.

Jennifer (Jen) Stroud — Daughter of the Animalville veterinarians, Dr. Tom and Dr. Angie Stroud; the older sister of Cody, Jennifer is one of the humans who knows about the Zoonauts and Animalville, but is not allowed to tell anyone.

Kongo the Gorilla—One of the leaders of the Zoonauts, along with Laika. Theoretical physicist, supergizmo designer, robotics expert, and financial specialist, Kongo is the Zoonauts financial advisor. He secures investments for the funding and operation of Animalville. Father to Patty Cake, Kongo arrived in Animalville in 1987 after a shuttle flight. He has remarkable scientific ability, an IQ of 200, and the special ability to "step outside of time."

Kornblend — An Alien Amadorian pilot whose mission, along with Fishwick, is to bring back Laika the Russian Dog alive to Amador.

Laika the Russian Dog — A Siberian husky named after the first Russian dog that went into space in 1957. Laika speaks fluent English and is one of the Zoonaut leaders in Animalville. Laika's special power is the ability to project a protective shield.

Ling-Ling the Panda — A Chinese Panda who can detect the mental thoughts of Amadorians and track their travels from Amador, which is more than four light years away.

Major Davis Prescott—The new Security and Liaison Officer at Site Lucky Bravo Lucky (also known as Animalville), an expert pilot. He is instrumental in rescuing Patty Cake, Jennifer, Cody, and Laika from an Alien attack on their aircraft.

Major Mike McIntosh — The first human to speak with Methuselah the Senegalese Parrot. Major Mike learned how the yellow light changed the animals. A Korean War veteran, he was put in charge of Space Animal Research and took care of the Zoonauts until he passed away; also known as General Mike.

Methuselah — The eighty-year-old, talking Senegal Gray Parrot has an IQ of 145 and is the oldest Zoonaut. He is Major Mike's best friend who was changed by the Alien yellow light in 1952 and as a result became much smarter; he remembers all he sees, since memory is his gift. Methuselah is the Zoonauts' historian for Animalville.

Miss Baker the Squirrel Monkey — A Zoonaut that can disarm bombs and is handy with a wrench. Her character is based on a participant in the US Space Program who was called America's "First Lady in Space."

Mungo the Parrot— Mungo the Senegal Parrot is a natural linguist. He can grasp any language he hears and speak it immediately. He is fascinated with voices, television, the Internet, and anything else involving communication. His IQ is 152.

Patty Cake the Gorilla—Daughter of Kongo, she has the ability to move herself (psychokinesis) and objects (telekinesis) using only her mental powers. She has the power to "Far-See," i.e., she can focus on a person or object that is distant or out of sight.

Percy the Orangutan Pilot, also known as "Race"— One of the Zoonauts who insists everyone call him "Race," after the much admired cartoon character he emulates since he has learned to fly. Race is a rescue helicopter pilot who teaches Cough Drop to fly.

Professor Mutzie the French Poodle — One of the Zoonauts and an inventor of the mechanized voice box, the "voder circuit," or "mic," that when implanted, enables the Zoonauts to speak English.

Sarafina Flores Abaroa — Jennifer's Mexican-American friend who has special abilities that help the Zoonauts in their defense of the humans against the Amadorians; Sara's father, with Kongo and Dr. Tom Stroud, helped establish Abaroatraonics to fund the Zoonauts and operations at Animalville.

Tre-Pok — The Chief Warlord of Amador and the Commander of Fishwick and Kornblend who threatens to turn the scout pilots into luggage if they fail in their mission to bring back the Russian Dog Laika alive.

"Who is your favorite Zoonaut?"

Visit the Zoonauts online at www.zoonauts.com
Follow us on Twitter and Like us on Facebook.

Printed in the United States
By Bookmasters